New Year's Kiss

NEW YEAR'S KISS

LEE MATTHEWS

Underlined

Text copyright © 2020 by Kieran Viola
Cover art copyright © 2020 by Jeff Ostberg

Visit us on the Web! GetUnderlined.com

Educators and librarians, for a variety of teaching tools, visit us at RHTeachersLibrarians.com

Library of Congress Cataloging-in-Publication Data
Names: Matthews, Lee, author.
Title: New Year's kiss / Lee Matthews.
Description: First edition. | New York : Underlined, [2020] | Audience: Ages 12 and up. |
Summary: Shy, straight-laced Tess meets Christopher while spending Christmas break at her grandmother's Vermont lodge, and he agrees to help her complete her bucket list before New Year's Eve.
Identifiers: LCCN 2020004027 (print) | LCCN 2020004028 (ebook) |
ISBN 978-0-593-17985-7 (trade paperback) | ISBN 978-0-593-17986-4 (ebook)
Subjects: CYAC: Dating (Social customs)—Fiction. | Sisters—Fiction. | Lists—Fiction. |
Grandmothers—Fiction. | Inns—Fiction.
Classification: LCC PZ7.1.M3784 New 2020 (print) | LCC PZ7.1.M3784 (ebook) |
DDC [Fic]—dc23

The text of this book is set in 11-point Adobe Caslon.
Interior design by Ken Crossland

Printed in the United States of America
10 9 8 7 6 5 4 3 2 1
First Edition

For my boys

CHAPTER ONE

DECEMBER 26

"It looks like a drunk elf threw up in here."

I snorted a laugh and looked at my sister, Lauren, as we stopped just inside the sliding glass doors to the Evergreen Lodge. Lauren was not wrong. The huge, three-story lobby atrium, with its exposed wood beams and tremendous chandeliers (made of a thousand fake deer antlers), was still decorated for Christmas—and the sensory experience was an onslaught of yuletide cheer. Every one of the beams was swagged with evergreen garland and roped with white twinkle lights. The chandeliers had been draped in red-and-green-plaid ribbon, and large glass balls hung overhead. Christmas-themed pillows overflowed from every couch and chair, and there were Christmas trees of all sizes everywhere. In the corners, on the counters, acting as centerpieces for the low coffee tables. There was even a life-sized animatronic Santa next to the check-in desk, waving with one hand and holding a plate of cookies in the other, while the instrumental soundtrack to *The Nutcracker* played at a respectful volume from hidden surround-sound speakers.

"Why does the elf have to be drunk?" I asked.

Lauren rolled her eyes like I was *so* lame. Which, let's be honest, I should be used to by now. But my cheeks went ahead and started burning anyway. Lauren pretty much always thought I was lame. I wasn't sure why I kept trying. If there was one thing for certain on this earth, it was that my big sister and I did *not* share the same sense of humor. Or style. Or basic outlook on life. And still . . .

"No, seriously," I said. "Couldn't the elf just have the flu? Or E. coli?"

"Ew!" Lauren scrunched her perfect nose. "That's so gross."

"How is throwing up from the flu grosser than throwing up from being drunk? Barf is barf."

"Why do you always do this?" Lauren asked.

I have no idea, I thought.

"Do what?" I said.

"Overanalyze everything. It was just an offhanded joke. God, Tess. Just chill."

Lauren sighed the sigh of the world-weary and looked at her phone, punching in a message with her thumbs before shoving it back into the pocket of her tight jeans. The second she looked up, she shouted "Loretta!" and raised her arm straight up in the air. Her smile even seemed genuine, which was impressive, considering Lauren had spent the entire shuttle ride over from the tiny regional airport bitching about how our grandmother—who had insisted we call her Loretta from the day each of us could talk—hadn't sent a car. Instead, we had been jammed into the back of the twelve-seat Evergreen Lodge minibus with ten other ski-obsessed Vermont vacationers, all of whom had been in far better, louder, and even singier moods than we had. "Twelve Days of Christmas" was going to be playing on repeat in my head until basically the end of time.

"Girls!" Loretta called, walking over to us in her high heels and pencil skirt. Her chic steel-gray bob gleamed under the lights, and her makeup was, as always, perfectly applied—cheekbones defined, lips outlined, eyelashes long and curled. She air-kissed first Lauren, then me—enveloping us in a cloud of her rose-scented perfume—then stepped back to look us over.

Loretta was wearing a white silk shirt, a pearl choker, and tasteful diamond earrings. She looked like a million bucks, as usual. I tugged at the frayed cuffs of my sweatshirt and wondered if any of my friends' grandmothers made them feel frumpy and unstylish like mine did. Wasn't it supposed to be the other way around? My other grandma—Nana, my mom's mom—was twenty pounds heavier than Loretta, wore nothing but colorful cotton sweaters and jeans, and smelled of apple pie and Bengay. *She* made me feel ready for Fashion Week.

Not that I had put in maximum effort this morning. The day after the worst Christmas ever, and I was getting on a plane with my sister to enjoy a week of exile. If any day had ever screamed "comfy sweats," it was this one.

"Oh, it's good to see you both," Loretta said. "How was your trip?"

"It was fine," I told her just as Lauren said, "It was long." This was true. We'd had to fly from Philadelphia to Boston, hang out in the airport there for over an hour, and then board the tiny plane over to the Stowe airport, where we'd gotten on the musical shuttle bus. But I'd never been one to complain.

"Well, you're here now. Just wait until you see all the incredible events the staff has planned for this week. You girls are going to have such a fabulous time."

Lauren looked at me out of the corner of her eye, and I had to look away to keep from laughing again. There was always a litany of "incredible events" planned at Evergreen Lodge. My dad's family had run the place for generations, with Loretta at the helm now. The lodge was more like a compound, consisting of the main building with its huge lobby, event spaces, restaurants and coffee bar, indoor pool, fully equipped gym, and one hundred hotel-style rooms. But it didn't end there. Several outbuildings housed a spa, a greenhouse, a boathouse, a wedding chapel, a dance hall, a couple dozen private cabins, and the Little Green Lodge at the top of the ski lifts where people could rest and get hot chocolate and snacks between runs. Plus there was a staff of hundreds, each with their own specialty, whether it be lifeguarding, line-dancing, or fireside storytelling. Loretta knew every member of the staff by name and treated them all like family. Which was to say, she smiled at them occasionally.

Evergreen Lodge reminded me of this movie called *Dirty Dancing*, which my mom had made both me and Lauren watch the second we turned twelve. It had been Mom's favorite movie as a kid, and sometimes I wondered if that movie was the entire reason my mother had fallen in love with my dad. She must have walked into Evergreen Lodge the first time and envisioned Baby and Johnny doing their iconic lift in the center of the lobby and just said, *That's it! I'm in!* Of course, Mom and Dad's romance hadn't worked out quite as well as the one depicted in the movie. My parents were currently in the midst of finalizing their divorce. Which was the entire reason Lauren and I were here. Usually we came in the summer, because my mom liked hiking better than skiing, but we'd been here a few times in February so that Lauren and I could learn to ski, which was one of my dad's favorite things. This was the first time I had seen the place all done up for the holidays, though. Normally, I loved Christmas and would relish this cozy, merry atmosphere. With the way things were in my life right now, though, I was not in the mood.

Christmas was over, and I sort of wished the staff had already de-merried the place.

A family of four walked through the doors behind us, toting their skis and snowboards, the parents laughing and holding hands with ruddy faces and windswept hair. My heart panged. How could people be walking around all happy and carefree when everything was falling apart?

"Let's get you two settled," Loretta said, clasping her hands. She pivoted on her heel and led us across the lobby. "I've reserved one of the bigger rooms on the third floor for you. It has fantastic views of the mountains and the lake—not that I expect you'll be spending much time in your room, what with everything going on around the resort."

"Wait. *Our* room?" Lauren said. "As in *one* room?"

"Yes, I reserved just the one this time," Loretta said, glancing back over her shoulder at us with an expression that told us there would be no arguments. "Your parents thought it would be good for the two of you to spend some time together. You know, family time."

Heat flared through my entire body. How hypocritical could our parents be? Right now, at this very moment, they were literally splitting up our family. They had shipped us off the day after Christmas for the express purpose of dividing their things, boxing up my dad's stuff, *moving him out*. Because of them, there would never be *family time* again. So why did Lauren and I have to suffer?

"You've got to be kidding me," Lauren scoffed. "Do you have any idea how hypocritical that is?"

"Lauren!" I scolded under my breath, though I was more annoyed that my sister had the guts to say what I didn't.

"What? You know it's true," Lauren said as we stepped into the elevator. There was a giant wreath hung on the back wall, full of glittering berries and fake cardinals. An instrumental version of "It's Beginning to Look a Lot Like Christmas" played through the overhead speakers.

Loretta hit the button for the third floor and sniffed. "Girls, whatever your thoughts on your parents' current situation, you must understand this is difficult for them, too. They're both doing the best they can."

If throwing us out and forcing us to share the same room for a week is the best they can do, then we have serious problems, I thought.

I glanced at Loretta. Maybe I could ask my grandmother if I could come live with her. Maybe if I spent my last year and a half of high school with Loretta, I'd become poised and sophisticated by osmosis. And one day I could take over Evergreen Lodge and run the ice-skating competitions each January and the s'mores-and-scares campfire nights at Halloween, and the movies under the stars on summer weekends.

Loretta looked back at me. "We should get you an appointment at the salon while you're here, Tess. I don't know what's going on with that hair."

Lauren laughed.

Or maybe not.

6

...

It wasn't as if I didn't want to be more like my sister. In certain ways, anyway. I would have killed to have that seemingly effortless beauty of hers—to look fresh-faced and pretty without a hair out of place at all times—but for me, it was just impossible. Lauren took after our mom, having inherited her gorgeous olive complexion, lustrous dark hair, and natural curves. I, however, looked just like our Irish dad, with skin so white I practically glowed in the dark and very blah dark blond hair. Even on those rare days when I did manage to get my perfectly straight locks to look sleek and healthy before leaving the house, by the time I hit the bathroom after homeroom it was all piece-y and lanky and just hung there. While Lauren walked around looking like she had just stepped off a yacht somewhere in the Greek isles, I looked more like I'd just come from the potato fields and a hard day's work.

Such was the genetic roulette wheel, I guessed. I mean, we'd learned all about it in bio at the beginning of the year. I knew it was no one's fault. But that didn't change the fact that it sucked. And it sucked even harder that my dear old grandmother felt the need to point out my flaws. Especially when those very flaws had come from *her* side of the family, thank you very much.

"You two get settled and I'll see you down in the Antelope Room for dinner in a bit."

"Thanks, Loretta," I said gamely as our grandmother silently closed the door.

Lauren tossed her suitcase onto the double bed nearer the bathroom and groaned. "I can*not* believe we have to share a room for the next week." She pulled out her phone and started texting. "No offense."

I rolled my eyes and wheeled my suitcase over to the dresser to start unpacking my clothes. Even when we were on vacation, I liked to feel settled and organized, while Lauren preferred to live out of her suitcase like she was already on her planned gap year in Europe, where she intended to stay at Airbnbs or with any friends lucky enough to be studying abroad freshman year and "live life like it was intended to be lived," whatever that meant. I couldn't even imagine flying to a foreign country by myself, let alone cobbling together an itinerary *and* finding ways to earn money on the fly. I'd started babysitting the second I was old enough and had been stashing away twenty percent of everything I made ever since, saving up for college textbooks. My parents were always moaning and groaning about how paying for college wasn't about just the tuition but all the living expenses and supplies—especially the books. The way they talked, you'd think textbooks were all made of diamonds and gold.

I had no idea whether my parents' divorce was going to affect the family's money situation, or Lauren's and my college funds, but there was no way I was not going away to school. If there was anything I could do to help make it happen, I would. Traveling the world was all well and good for Lauren, but I was about schedules and goals and ticking off syllabus boxes. I couldn't wait to be in a place where everyone was focused on learning.

Once I'd gotten everything neatly placed inside the dresser, I zipped up my suitcase again, shoved it in a corner, and turned to gaze out the huge picture window overlooking the grounds. The sun was just setting over the mountains, turning the winter sky the most intense shade of pink I'd ever seen. Just below, dozens of people skated around the frozen lake, little kids grabbing onto parents' legs, older kids chasing one another and biffing spectacularly. A couple near the center held hands and twirled in a fast circle, using centrifugal force to keep them going. It was all very pretty, so I took a deep breath and attempted to smile. Unfortunately, I couldn't quite pull it off.

Irritated, I yanked the heavy curtains closed. That was when I spotted a printed schedule on the polished oak desk, a piece of furniture they'd stuck in every room, I supposed because of all the business retreats the lodge hosted. With a glance, I saw that it was a calendar of all the events Loretta had alluded to in the lobby. Everything from a timed snowman-building competition to a snowshoe race. Certain items had been highlighted in green, with a little *M* written next to them in Loretta's stiff handwriting. It was a lovely schedule, really—color-coded by age range for each event with the start and end times indicated. Just my kind of document.

"What do you think this means?" I asked, walking over to Lauren's bed. My sister was now kicked back against the pillows, watching music videos on YouTube.

"What?" Lauren asked without moving her eyes off the screen.

I grabbed her phone—"Hey!" she yelled—and shoved the paper in front of her face.

"This. What do you think the *M*s mean?"

Lauren snatched the page from my hand and scanned it, squinting. "International Buffet, New Year's Eve Teen Dance, Campfire Bingo . . . all marked with an *M*." She slapped the paper down dramatically and looked up at me. "You don't think she means *mandatory*, do you?"

"Oh, no. No way," I said. "I plan to spend the next six days in this room, reading and watching TV."

"There's a shock," Lauren said sarcastically.

"You're the one who was just watching YouTube!" I shot back.

"I was relaxing for five minutes, not hermit-ing myself away for *days*." Lauren got up and pulled off her sweater, which she tossed onto the floor in a heap. "I'm going to get out of here as soon as possible. But if Loretta thinks it's going to be so I can . . . 'build gingerbread houses,'" she read off the list, making a disgusted face, "she's out of her mind."

Actually, building gingerbread houses sounded kind of fun. My dad and I used to make them every Christmas when I was little—from a kit, but still. I loved planning out the decorations for our house and using the squeeze bag of icing to attach the candies (the ones I didn't eat). Suddenly I missed my dad so much my chest hurt.

Why was Mom making him leave? Why couldn't she just try harder?

"I don't know what your problem is," Lauren said, looking over the calendar again. "Don't you just *love* to have every moment of your life scheduled?"

Okay. She had a point. If I were in any mood for festive holiday fun, I would be all about this calendar of events, especially the mandatory parts. Honestly, even as I stood there, the idea was beginning to grow on me. If my grandmother wanted us at these things, we should go. I was sure she had her reasons.

"Mom says hi and have fun, by the way," Lauren said, handing the paper back to me and holding up her phone to show me her messages. "She said answer your texts, too."

I had turned my phone off as soon as we'd left our house in Philly that morning and hadn't turned it on since. I didn't want to talk to my mom. I didn't really feel like talking to anyone. Except my dad, suddenly. I rummaged through my backpack for my phone and powered it up. There were a bunch of texts from my friends, wishing me a good trip or asking what I'd gotten for Christmas. Then there were five texts from my mother—all checking-in kinds of things—and one from my dad. He'd sent me a picture of a heart someone had drawn in the snow on a mailbox. My own heart panged.

I texted him back.

Good one. Twenty points.

He immediately sent me a thumbs-up and a kissy emoji. Me and my dad had been sending each other random hearts we found in the world ever since I first got my phone in middle school. My father traveled a lot for work—he was legal counsel for a midsized boutique hotel chain called Galileo Properties that had locations all over the world—and it was a fun way for us to stay connected even if he was in Bali or Belgium or Canada somewhere. We'd only instituted the point system when we'd had a mock fight over whose find on a particular fall day had been cooler—the yellow heart-shaped leaf I had found in the backyard or the heart someone had drawn in the dust on a Jeep parked outside a hotel in Australia along with the words *Love is messy*. The highest a heart could score was twenty-five points. I was being a little generous with my score for the snow heart, but I was in a generous mood. When it came to my dad, anyway.

I put my phone away without texting Mom and looked at the schedule. "Well, our mandatory International Buffet Dinner is in fifteen minutes."

"Yeah, there's no way I'm going to that," Lauren said, back on her phone. "I wonder if there's any place around here that has good tapas." She opened Yelp and started typing.

There was a peppy knock on the door. Lauren and I exchanged a questioning look, and then she shoved herself off the bed and opened the door without even checking the peephole. The girl was going to get us killed one of these days, for sure.

"Hello. I'm Tarek. You must be Tess."

The guy standing in the hallway didn't look like a serial killer. He looked like the lead in a Hallmark Christmas movie. Except younger. He had broad shoulders, a thick head of brown hair, and eyes so blue I could tell they were blue even from across the room. He wore a forest-green Evergreen Lodge polo and black jeans that looked really good on him.

Lauren laughed. "Um, no. That's Tess. I'm Lauren. The pretty one."

Seriously? But Tarek just smiled. And it was a killer smile. Ugh. Lauren was a goner for sure. She fell in love at least once a day.

"I like your confidence," he said. "Well, it's nice to meet you, Lauren." He glanced over at me. "I guess that makes *you* Tess."

"Got it in one," I said.

"Nice to meet you both," he said politely. "Mrs. Sachs sent me to escort you down to our famous annual International Buffet Dinner."

"Great," I said. "I'm ready. Have fun with your tapas, Lauren!"

I made a move for the door, but Lauren stepped between me and Tarek. "Actually, I changed my mind. I had no idea this buffet thing was *famous*. How could I miss that?"

Shocker. Obviously, now that there was a hot guy involved, Lauren was in.

"Just give me five minutes to get ready," she told Tarek. Then she placed one hand on his chest and literally shoved him into the hallway. Tarek laughed.

"All right, then. I guess I'll just be waiting out here."

"Yeah, you will!" Lauren gave him a finger wave and closed the door. Then she turned to look at me, her mouth open. *Oh my God,* she whispered. "Did you *see* that guy?"

"I was standing right here," I said.

But Lauren was already in the bathroom, running the water, scrubbing her face, as if I didn't even exist.

CHAPTER TWO

"You're kidding me, right?" Lauren said as I slid into the chair next to hers at the long table we were sharing with Tarek and a bunch of random strangers. The Antelope Room was the buffet-style casual restaurant set at the back of the lodge, overlooking the award-winning gardens. Gardens that were bare right now, except for the dozens of intricate ice sculptures that dotted the empty flower beds, each lit with a spotlight that made it seem to glow from the inside out. The carvers had decorated the courtyard with everything from skiing snowmen to frolicking deer to—yes—a giant antelope, and a couple dozen kids were gathered at the windows, staring outside.

"That's all you're eating?" Lauren asked me. Accused me, really.

"Yeah, Tess, you should try something else," Tarek offered, mouth half full. "They've been working on this menu for months."

That was not a surprise. Each of the buffet stations—set up as always at one end of the large room—had been designated for a different country and was decorated with flags and posters and random paraphernalia to represent the culture. It was all very impressive, but it wasn't going to turn me suddenly into an adventurous eater. Apparently Tarek was no longer on the clock, because he was busy digging into a plate piled high with a random selection of food. The girl sitting across from us glanced up, looked at my plate—hers was already picked clean—then looked down into her lap again. She was about my age with light brown skin and curly black hair, and was wearing a colorfully striped ski hat. Inside.

"What?" I replied under my breath to Lauren. "You know I don't like spicy food."

"Okay, but not everything up there is spicy. There are, like, a hundred dishes representing dozens of countries and you got the lamest thing you could find." The whole concept of the international buffet had really grown on Lauren in the ten minutes since she'd decided to attend. She used chopsticks to pick up some kind of orangey-brown meat, like using chopsticks was something she'd been born knowing how to do. "You could at least try something new every once in a while."

"I *am* trying something new. I've never had pineapple on chicken before."

"Oooh. What're you going to do next? Order non-plain pizza?" Lauren rolled her eyes, popped the piece of meat into her mouth, then turned her attention to Tarek, who was on her other side, and commenced her flirting ritual, which involved a ton of hair tossing and loud laughing. I looked down at the pineapple grilled chicken and white rice on my plate and suddenly felt very, very dull. I speared one of the pineapple pieces with my fork and ate it grumpily. Where the hell was Loretta, anyway? Was she going to show up to eat this "mandatory" dinner with us or what? And if not, how was I supposed to get credit for being here?

I cut into the chicken and looked around the table. The

Antelope Room was roughly half the size of my high school cafeteria back home, with long, picnic-style tables running down its center to encourage conversation and friend-making among the guests. There were also smaller tables and booths set up around the perimeter in case families preferred their privacy. Like the lobby, the room was decked out for Christmas, with red and green felt runners down the centers of the tables and bowls full of pine cones and ornaments used as decoration. There was a family with three little kids at one end of our table, a group of friends passing around videos on their phones, the girl with the hat across from me—who appeared to be reading a book in her lap—and a few empty chairs on Tarek's far side. I wished I'd thought to bring my book. I was supposed to be reading *Sense and Sensibility* over break for extra credit in English class, but I hadn't gotten very far before Christmas, so I'd set a goal of seventy-five pages per day for the next week. I'd read today's seventy-five on the two planes, but if I'd brought it down with me, I could have gotten a jump start on tomorrow's chunk, which would have been good because (A) who knew how much stuff Loretta was going to make us do tomorrow, and (B) clearly Lauren was bent on ignoring me in favor of Mr. Shoulders over there.

What was weird was, the girl with the book didn't seem to be related to the family, and she hadn't so much as glanced at Tarek. What was she doing at our table? Who was she here with?

A normal person would have simply asked, but I was not a normal person. I had a serious problem when it came to talking to strangers, in that I was completely incapable of doing it. My throat closed every time I tried. What if the person didn't want to be interrupted? Or what if they found me completely uninteresting or annoying? This girl, for example, seemed utterly engrossed in whatever she was reading. If I tried to talk to her, she'd probably give me a curt answer and then turn away, and then I'd have to spend the rest of the meal feeling awkward and avoiding eye contact.

Yes, this was how my mind worked. I didn't like it, but there didn't seem to be anything I could do to change it.

Then the girl shifted in her seat and lifted the book to rest it on the table. I almost gasped. It was *The Seven Siren Stars*. One of my all-time favorites. I'd just read the sequel with my book club back home.

This was a sign. I *had* to say something. With Loretta MIA and Lauren otherwise occupied, it wasn't like I had anyone else to talk to. I was just about to give it a go, when my sister got up from the table.

"See you later, loser," Lauren said under her breath.

Then she followed Tarek toward the door.

"What? Where're you going?" I demanded, dropping my fork with a clatter.

Lauren didn't answer. She simply took Tarek's hand as they started speed-walking, giggling their way free of the dinner buffet.

Something inside me snapped. White-hot heat enveloped me. Lauren couldn't just abandon me. We were supposed to be having family time. This thing was mandatory! Did Lauren not understand the definition of the word? Considering how many classes she skipped, probably not. But still. I shoved away from the table and followed my sister, adrenaline fueling my every step.

"Hey!" I shouted the second we were free of the room. "Lauren, stop!"

Finally, Lauren did stop, tipping her face toward the lofty ceiling of the lobby in frustration. She let go of Tarek, who kept walking, and turned on me with a sour expression that I knew very well. It was her *don't mess with me, little sister* face. "What?" she snapped.

"Where're you going?" I said through my teeth, glancing around to check that no one was watching us. All I saw were families, groups, and couples laughing and traipsing from event to event, enjoying this last vacation of the year. Oh, how I wished I could be one of them.

"Tarek's friends are meeting up in town," Lauren informed me, gesturing toward the door where Tarek stood typing on his phone. "He's calling an Uber now so we can go."

"You can't just go. Loretta will freak."

Lauren turned up her palms. "Do you even *see* Loretta? She didn't bother to show up, so why should I stick around?"

I couldn't argue with that. It was sort of amazing how much Lauren and I thought alike, considering how different we were. It was like we had the same thoughts but processed them in exactly the opposite ways.

"Also, have you met me?" Lauren added. "I don't give a crap if she freaks."

"Car'll be here in five minutes," Tarek interjected, pocketing his phone as he walked over.

Lauren turned to go, but I was still angry. The very thought of my sister getting to do whatever she wanted while I toed the line, as always, pissed me right off. I lunged for Lauren's hand just as we passed by a big circle of cushy chairs set around the roaring stone fireplace near the center of the lobby.

Now Lauren was pissed off, too. "Will you stop? You're embarrassing me. And yourself. Not that that's anything new."

My face stung. Why did Lauren always have to be so mean to me? We were only two years apart, but sometimes Lauren treated me like I was ten years old and wanted to play Barbies or something.

"We're supposed to stay together," I reminded her.

Lauren crossed her arms over her chest and smiled a slow, sly smile. "Fine," she said, then paused. "So come with me."

My insides froze. Go *with* her? To meet up with strangers and do who knew what? In the middle of nowhere? I felt my face go pale. Lauren laughed. "See? You're such a goody-goody. You never say yes to *anything*. And I already told you I'm not spending this whole vacation holed up in our room."

Tarek, who was by the door a few yards away, called, "Lauren, you coming?"

"I'll tell Mom and Dad," I heard myself threaten. Okay. So maybe I *was* ten years old.

Lauren frowned. "There *is* no Mom and Dad anymore. And me going to some random party is the last thing they care about right now anyway. So stop being a baby and go do what you do best. Go be a loner." My eyes burned with tears as my sister turned away, and then my heart leapt pathetically when she turned back again. "And if you tell Loretta I left, you're dead."

And then she was gone. My hands balled into fists as tears threatened to overwhelm me. Lauren was *so* awful. How could she just leave me here by myself? With everything else going on? I thought big sisters were supposed to, like, take care of their younger siblings. Not walk out on them like everyone else seemed to be doing. *Maybe I should just go back to my room, pack up my stuff, and disappear,* I thought. It wasn't as if anyone would have noticed.

"Wow." A low male voice interrupted my downward spiral. "That was unnecessarily harsh."

. . .

The boy was cute. No, *cute* didn't cover it. He was YouTube—star worthy. And not just *I made this video in my backyard and almost broke my neck so I got a million likes* cute, but *I have my own channel and product and entourage* cute. All these things considered, I kind of couldn't believe he was talking to me, and suddenly I was blushing again. Big-time. And then I uttered a brilliant and witty comeback that I was sure I would remember for the rest of my days: "Um . . . yeah."

I ducked my head, tucking my hair behind one ear, and turned to go. I didn't want this hot stranger seeing me burst into tears on top of everything else I'd endured today.

"Was that your sister?"

My back to him now, I took a deep breath. I could pretend I didn't hear him, walk away, and put an end to the misery that was this night, or I could do the opposite of that. I could turn around and answer him. For some reason, maybe because the adrenaline from my fight with Lauren was still coursing through my veins, I chose option B.

"Yes, that was my sister."

"You're not gonna, like, do what she told you to do, are you?" he asked, swinging his long blond bangs away from his brow to reveal green eyes that were unlike any I'd ever seen. "Because that doesn't seem like the best way to get your revenge."

I smirked. Couldn't help it. "Who says I want revenge?"

"Your face does. It's written all over it."

"And you know my face so well," I joked.

Wait, was I being witty? With a guy?

"I like to think I do," he shot back. "I mean, we have all this history."

Now I smiled for real. I approached the couch where he was sitting, and only then did I notice that his right leg was in a cast from the knee down, stretched the length of the Christmas-red cushions. He had an iPad, a phone, and a stack of books on the table next to him.

"Whoa. What happened?" I asked.

He lifted one shoulder and knocked on his cast. "Didn't you hear? It was all over the news this morning."

"What?" I asked, intrigued, sitting in the armchair closest to him. Maybe he *was* internet famous.

"Yesterday on the slopes there was this kid, maybe seven years old, and he just slipped out of the chair lift," he said, pushing himself up slightly to sit straighter against the arm of the couch. "His dad was right next to him, and he said it was like one second his kid was there, and the next second nothing but air."

"Oh my God!" I covered my mouth with both hands. "He fell?"

"No. That's the crazy thing. He managed to grab the foot bar as he went down. So there he is, dangling like twenty-five feet above the snow, and me and my friends were on a snowboard run, and we saw him. So we got a bunch of people to take off their jackets, and we tied them together to make a big blanket, and then we held it underneath the ski lift *just* as the kid fell."

"No way!"

"Yes way."

"So . . . did you catch him? Is he okay? And how did your leg get broken?"

"Oh, he's okay. But our positioning was all wrong and he kind of fell on top of me. That's how I broke my leg."

"That's unreal."

"Yeah, it totally is." He paused and smiled widely at me. "Because it's actually not even a little bit true."

My jaw dropped. I didn't know whether to scream, laugh, or hit the guy. "You made it up?"

He lifted one shoulder. "It's better than the real story."

"Which is?"

"Some idiot shoved me into a nasty patch of ice on a snowboard run on Christmas morning, and I ran into a tree and ended up in the hospital."

I swatted his arm.

"Ow! Hey!" He covered the spot I'd hit with one hand, as if I'd actually hurt him. "You can't beat on the injured."

"You may be injured, but you're also a big fat liar," I said with a laugh. I sat back again, the crackling fire warming the left side of my face. "Seriously, though. Good story. You should tell that to everyone."

"Oh, I have been. People around here are calling me a hero. One lady even brought me cake." He gestured at a plate full of yellow crumbs.

I laughed again and shook my head at him. It felt good to laugh for real. It was something I hadn't done in a long time.

"I felt so guilty I told her the truth. But she let me keep it anyway."

"She did?"

He raised his palms. "Said she appreciates a good storyteller. So. What's your deal? Why was your sister all over you like that?"

I shot him a dubious glance. "You really want to know?"

"I've literally got nothing else going on." He looked me up and down. "Unless . . . you also brought me cake."

I raised my hands to indicate my utter lack of cake, but I kind of wished I had some. I hadn't exactly eaten much at dinner, and now my stomach grumbled. But I supposed I could deal with that later. "Sorry. Well, if I'm going to tell you my sob story, you better tell me your name first."

"I'm Christopher Callahan," he said, and reached out a hand.

I shook it, and my mouth went dry. Total arm tingles. Tingles everywhere, actually. A slight blush rose on Christopher's face and he held my gaze, the long lashes on those green-green eyes fluttering slightly. He had the tiniest bit of sunburn on his otherwise perfect nose.

"Tess Sachs," I replied.

And then I told him everything.

CHAPTER THREE

I basically floated back to my room. Christopher and I had spent two hours chatting and watching videos on his computer before his mother came along and introduced herself to me, then told Christopher he needed his rest. She thanked me for keeping her "daredevil kid" company, then produced a wheelchair and carted him back to his room. But before that happened, it was basically the best conversation I'd ever had. Christopher was amazing. He was funny and kind and a good listener. He never interrupted my stories to tell one of his own. It was all so easy but at the same time so exciting. Because basically every time he looked at me, I melted. It would have been embarrassing if there had been anyone I knew around to witness it.

There was also the fact that Christopher was, well, beautiful. Way better looking than Tarek. Half the time we were together, I had been checking the door to see if Lauren had come back yet. I one hundred percent enjoyed hanging out with Christopher, but if Lauren saw us together, it would be like winning bonus points. Unfortunately, Lauren had never come back. In fact, it was after ten and she *still* wasn't back, which was totally against Loretta's house rules. Lauren was going to be in big trouble if Loretta found out.

But then, the chances Loretta *would* find out were slim to none. I hadn't seen my grandmother once all night, even though she'd mandated that we attend that particular dinner, going so far as to send one of her employees to make sure we got there. Why hadn't she shown up? When Lauren and I had looked over the schedule she'd left for us, we'd both assumed that if something was mandatory, that meant she would be there, too.

Maybe she was counting on Tarek to keep an eye on us tonight. Loretta's employees were nothing if not loyal. Was it possible that Tarek would tell Loretta we'd both bailed on dinner? He wouldn't have to confess his own involvement if he didn't want to.

I tugged out my phone to text my sister a warning but then heard Lauren's voice in my head telling me what a goody-goody I was. Clenching my jaw, I shoved my phone back in my pocket. I'd have bet a million dollars that Lauren hadn't thought about the consequences of bailing once since she'd walked out the door.

"Not my problem," I said to myself.

I used my key card to enter our room and flopped down on my back in the middle of my bed, a huge smile on my face. I couldn't *stop* smiling. And it felt as if it had been months since I'd smiled at all. Christopher had done this to me. He'd made me feel special. He'd made me feel *seen*. Most guys—hell, most *people*—always seemed to be looking around to see if there was anyone better or cooler to talk to, or worse—texting better, cooler people on their phones. I mean, I had friends, don't get me wrong, but it was a small circle, and we weren't exactly rolling in the cool party invites. But Christopher had been utterly focused on me. He'd commiserated when I'd told him about my parents and detailed how much

Christmas had sucked, knowing it was the last time we would all wake up on Christmas morning together, in our house. And why did Lauren have to be such a bitch? Wasn't divorce the sort of thing that was supposed to make siblings bond? Instead, Lauren seemed to get meaner by the day.

Christopher had listened to it all. And he hadn't looked at his phone once. Nor had he pointed out how much worse *his* Christmas morning had been than mine, which would have been completely valid, considering he'd broken his leg and ended up in the hospital.

Ugh. Maybe I had been a tad self-centered, actually. Tomorrow I would bring him some of that gingerbread cake from the Best Bean Café and ask him to tell me all about *his* sucky Christmas.

I had just sat up to get ready for bed when my phone rang. My heart sank when I saw the caller ID. It was my mother. I hesitated for half a second, then hit *Ignore.* If I talked to my mom right now, it would just ruin my good mood, and I'd earned a little bit of holiday cheer, hadn't I? My mother expected me to act like everything was normal and like she'd done nothing wrong, but it was such a lie. My mom was the whole reason my parents were getting divorced. For the past year, she'd been grumpy and surly and sometimes completely dismissive of my dad. Even on the nights when it was clear Dad was trying really hard to be sweet or romantic, like when he brought home flowers or ordered takeout so my mom wouldn't have to cook, it was like nothing registered with her. TV shows and commercials were always saying that marriage was hard work, but if that was the case, it seemed like my dad had done all the heavy lifting.

Maybe if my mom had tried, even a little, we wouldn't be going through all this heartache.

I changed into clean pajamas and brushed my teeth, looking into my eyes in the mirror and watching them shine every time I thought about Christopher. A giggle escaped through all the toothpaste foam. I couldn't help it. I wished I'd taken a picture of him so I could show it to Lauren when she finally got back. But maybe I could do one better and introduce the two of them tomorrow. Christopher had said he'd likely be in the same place all day while his parents visited friends nearby. He'd begged off due to his leg, and his parents seemed in the mood to let him have his way right now, what with the fact that his whole holiday break had been ruined. Not to mention his basketball season.

"A basketball player," I breathed as I crawled into bed. None of the basketball players at my school even knew I existed.

Before I turned out the light, I checked my phone one last time to see if my sister had texted, but there was nothing other than a new voice mail from my mom, which I also ignored. My head had just hit the pillow when there was a sharp rap on the door, and it opened.

I sat up in bed and yelped. Loretta stood there, backlit by the hallway lights.

"Loretta!" I blurted out in surprise. "What the—"

"Did you two leave dinner early?" Loretta flicked on the lights and blinked. She took in Lauren's empty bed and paled. "Where is your sister?" she demanded.

My shoulders tensed and my brain started to formulate a lie, but really, what good would it do? Nothing I could say would change the fact that Lauren was not here. And besides, I shouldn't *have* to lie for Lauren. Why was my sister always putting me in this position?

"I don't know," I said honestly.

"You don't *know*?" Loretta was incredulous.

"No!" I shouted, shocking even myself. "I *don't* know. She left, okay? And I don't know where she went. I'm not her keeper. And why are you yelling at *me*? I'm the one who's here, in my bed, where I'm supposed to be!"

Loretta relaxed her grip on the doorknob, stepped inside, and closed the door quietly behind her. Her posture completely changed as she lowered herself onto the edge of Lauren's bed, facing me. She looked small in that pose, and older somehow. "You're right. I'm sorry. I didn't realize I was yelling. It's simply that your parents asked me to take care of you, and I can't do that if you're out running around all over town."

"Well, again, *I* didn't go anywhere," I grumbled.

Loretta gave me a wan smile. "I apologize. And I'm sorry I couldn't make it to the dinner this evening. I did try. It's one of my favorite nights of the year. Unfortunately I was tied up with a legal matter that needed my immediate attention."

"Legal matter?" I asked. "That doesn't sound good."

She waved a hand dismissively, but I could tell something was up. "It will be fine. We have to deal with this sort of thing all the time. It's nothing to worry about."

I was about to ask for more info, and maybe even suggest she call my dad, when the door flew open and Lauren came whirling in. "Tess! You're never going to believe this! Adam Michel is going to be at the—"

She stopped in her tracks and went silent the second she saw Loretta.

"What about Adam Michel?" I asked, my pulse racing. Adam Michel was my favorite singer in the entire world. *Adam is going to be at the* what? But then Loretta stood up stiffly, and I knew that this was not the time.

"You *told* on me?" Lauren seethed, glaring at me. Her expression had morphed from excited to murderous in two point five seconds. Kind of impressive, actually.

"What!" I said. "No! She—"

"Then what is Loretta doing here?" Lauren snapped, throwing her bag into the corner, where half its contents spilled out. She, of course, didn't even seem to notice. "I didn't show up at ten on the dot, so you called her?"

"No! Oh my God. Why do you *always* blame me?" I shouted, throwing off my sheets and standing up. "I was just going to bed and she walked right in demanding to know where you were!"

Loretta let out a sharp whistle that brought both me and Lauren up short. We exchanged a look, like *what the hell was that?* As far as I could recall, Loretta had never whistled in her life.

"Excuse me, *she* is right here!" Loretta shouted. "And *she* would appreciate it if you'd stop talking about her like she is not."

Lauren shifted from foot to foot, looking at the carpet. My heart was pounding painfully.

"Now, you two listen to me and listen good." Loretta put her hands out, palms down. "This is *not* how this week is going to go. I will not have you fighting. You are my guests—*and* you represent this family and this hotel, and I expect you to behave as such." She leveled a threatening stare at each of us, first Lauren, then me. "From this moment on, you will stick to your schedule and you will not leave this property without running it by me first. Is that understood?"

Wow. Way to be a dictator, Grandma, I thought.

"Yes," I said quietly.

Lauren huffed and looked away.

"I said, *is that understood?*" Loretta demanded.

"Yes! Fine! Whatever!" Lauren groused, throwing her hands up and letting them slap back down at her sides. "Can we just go to bed now?"

"Yes, you may." Loretta kissed me on the forehead, then walked over to Lauren, who, shockingly, allowed Loretta to do the same to her. "Good night," Loretta said. Then she slipped out and closed the door silently behind her.

"Thanks a lot," Lauren grumbled in my direction. But there wasn't a ton of venom behind it this time, so instead of fighting her, I just got into bed and rolled over onto my side, turning my back to my sister. Lauren went into the bathroom, slammed the door, and turned on the shower full blast.

So much for telling Lauren all about Christopher and the butterflies he inspired. And what was all that about Adam Michel? I took a deep breath and huffed it out, staring at the closed curtains across the window, my pulse still racing. I tried to think about Christopher, to reignite that good mood I'd been in, like, five minutes ago. But it didn't work. There was no recovering from the wrath of my sister.

CHAPTER FOUR

DECEMBER 27

"I thought it might be nice for the three of us to go shopping for New Year's Eve dresses together," Loretta said as she spread jam onto a scone the next morning, "so I took this afternoon off."

I stopped with a forkful of pancakes halfway to my mouth. Shopping was so not my thing. But I was sure Lauren would be up for it. There wasn't a store my sister didn't love to raid or a wallet she didn't live to empty. But even Lauren groaned under her breath. Loretta shot her a half-admonishing, half-disappointed look, but my sister just slumped down farther in her chair. And she calls me the immature one.

"That sounds like fun," I said, forcing a smile. "I didn't bring any dresses, so I could definitely use something new."

"Well, I'm all good. I brought *tons* of dresses," Lauren said.

"Still, I think it would be nice for the three of us to go out together," Loretta said. "Lauren, you can help your sister choose something. And since when do you ever turn down free clothes?"

I smirked. Clearly Loretta had been paying attention. For the past ten or so years, Lauren had used every birthday and Christmas to get some sort of coat or boots or jewelry out of Loretta, who (A) seemed to have an endless cash flow, and (B) had impeccable taste. Which meant that it wasn't the prospect of shopping that was making Lauren groan; it was the prospect of spending time with me and Loretta.

"I'm going to go get some more bacon," I said, shoving my chair back from the table. I needed a breather from all this together time, especially if today was going to be nothing but that. On my way back up to the buffet, I saw Christopher and his parents enter the restaurant, Christopher balanced on a pair of crutches with his broken leg crooked beneath him. As if drawn by magnets, Christopher's eyes met mine, and he smiled. My heart flopped over and started panting. If possible, he was even better looking in the bright sunlight than he'd been last night.

Christopher paused to say something to his parents; then the two of them went over to the chef at the omelet station while Christopher made his way over to me on his crutches. He was wearing a red turtleneck under a flannel shirt, and his blond hair hung over one eye.

"Good morning," he said, and looked down at my empty plate. "Firsts or seconds?"

It took me a beat to comprehend the question, but then I laughed. "Oh, seconds. I need more bacon."

"Don't we all?" he joked.

"Well, actually, I didn't *need* more bacon. I just needed to get away from my family for five seconds." I cast a look over to the table where Loretta and Lauren were sitting, except Loretta was gone, her place cleaned, and Lauren was slumped down staring at her phone. *Look up,* I urged her silently. *See how not-lame I am over here talking to a cute guy.*

Lauren did not comply. Instead, she chuckled at something on her screen and began rapid-fire texting.

"I hear that," Christopher said. "Come on, let's get on line. I'm starved."

We made our way over to what I thought of as the Carb Section—where all the pancakes, French toast, waffles, and croissants were displayed. Christopher made a move to grab a plate, but it quickly became clear that there was no way for him to get food and maneuver with his crutches.

"I've got it," I offered, grabbing a plate for him. "Just tell me what you want."

"Thanks." He smiled a heart-stopping smile and tossed his long bangs out of his eyes. "Guess I'm going to need an assist at meals for a while."

I looked away before he could see my extreme blush. "You upgraded from the wheelchair, huh?"

Christopher looked down at one crutch, then the other. "Yeah. But these things are murder on my underarms, and I've already lost my balance a few times."

"You get used to it pretty quick. You'd be surprised." I reached for a pair of tongs. "Pancakes?"

"Sure." Christopher raised his eyebrows. "When were you on crutches?"

"Oh, I used to skateboard," I said, waving the tongs like it was no big deal. I put some syrup in a little cup and added it to the plate. "But then I broke my ankle attempting a three-sixty in a competition, and it was *not* pretty. I kind of quit after that."

My face flushed. I hated admitting that I'd quit. My father had tried so hard to get me back on the board, telling me it was heartbreaking to see me give up on something I loved so much. I felt the same way about my parents and their marriage.

"Do you want a waffle?"

"Uh, yes, please," Christopher replied. "And some of that strawberry sauce."

I piled it all onto the plate.

"Well. That sucks," Christopher said of my skateboarding injury. He looked me up and down quickly, as if trying to picture me on a skateboard. "When was this?"

"I was, like, ten," I said, trying to play it down. But I knew exactly how old I'd been. The accident had happened three days after my tenth birthday. I would never forget it. "No big deal, though. It wasn't like I was going to go pro or anything."

"Still, it stinks to have to give up something you're good at."

"Like you and basketball?"

"Yeah, but it's just for a season. I'll play spring ball for sure," he said, and I kind of loved how confident he was about it.

"You don't also want French toast, do you?" I said dubiously.

"What am I, crazy?" He paused. "Obviously I want French toast."

"Okay, this breakfast might kill you," I pointed out, slipping a couple of slices onto the top of his now teetering pile of food.

"We haven't even gotten to the meat and potatoes yet." He grinned.

"We're going to need another plate," I shot back with a laugh.

"Tess! There you are."

It was Loretta, approaching us with her high heels clicking.

"Oh, hi, Loretta. This is Christopher. He's a guest at the hotel. Christopher, this is my grandmother Loretta."

The two of them locked eyes, and something passed between them. It was obvious they'd met, and my grandmother looked almost . . . nervous? But before I could even figure it out, whatever I'd seen in her expression was gone, and she was back to normal Loretta mode.

"So, Tess. You didn't tell me last night that your family owns the great Evergreen Lodge empire," Christopher joked. "Were you just being modest?"

"It didn't come up." I looked back and forth between them. "Wait. So you two already know each other?"

"Yes. Yes, we do. I met Christopher and his parents at the front door when he returned from the hospital yesterday." She clasped her hands together. "I trust your new room is comfortable?"

"Very much so, thank you."

He plucked a slice of French toast from the top of the carb pile I was holding and took a bite, wobbling a bit on his crutches.

"And are your . . . parents in attendance this morning?" she asked, her lips tightening ever so slightly.

"Yes, they're over there getting their food." Christopher nodded toward his parents, who had reached the front of the line at the omelet station. His mother was talking to the chef while his father barked into his phone. My grandmother's eyes narrowed at the sight of them.

"Well, good. You enjoy your breakfast, and let us know if there's anything you need." Loretta pivoted slightly to look at me. "Now, I have a driver all ready to take us into town to do that shopping we talked about. We'll meet in the lobby at eleven. Then I thought

we'd have lunch at Le Grand Café and take in the new china exhibit at the museum."

"Chinese artwork?" I asked.

"No. China. As in dishware. It's supposed to be an extensive collection of pieces from throughout American history. I've been so looking forward to going, and now I have you two girls to accompany me!" She smiled and squeezed my arm. "Meet me at the private entrance in twenty minutes."

"Will do," I said with a smile. Loretta turned and strode away, greeting guests as she crossed the wide, crowded room. When she reached the omelet station, she exchanged a few words with Christopher's parents—all business, it seemed—and then checked her watch and hurried off.

"Wow."

"What?" I said, suddenly exhausted.

"You don't want to do any of that, do you?"

He had a genuinely curious look on his face. I tilted my head at him. "Do you want me to get you meat or not?"

"Yeah, I do. The question is, what do *you* want to do?"

I walked to the next station and started selecting food at random. A few slices of bacon, some sausage, some corned-beef hash.

"Okay. To answer your question, no. I don't want to do any of the things my grandmother has planned."

"But you're going to anyway?"

"Yep."

Christopher motor-boated his lips and looked off in the direction Loretta had disappeared. "Ya know, maybe your new year's resolution should be to not always do what's expected of you. You need to live a little."

God, this was humiliating. We'd had such a good time last night, and now he was going to leave this conversation thinking I was totally lame. "You sound like my sister," I said.

"Well. Nobody wants that," he joked.

I moved to the next station, even though both of the plates I was carrying were so full they couldn't exactly handle any more food. I was feeling antsy suddenly, and irritated. I turned to face Christopher, and he almost collided with me, saving himself by leaning heavily on his crutches.

"Look, she's my grandmother. She just wants to spend time with me. Is it wrong to do what she wants me to do? Is that so bad?"

"No, but you're on vacation, right? You should also do some things *you* want to do," he said. "And not just when you're on vacation. It's fun to be spontaneous once in a while. To, like, prove people wrong. Like you did with your sister last night."

"How did I prove my sister wrong last night?" I asked.

"You didn't go off to your room and act like a loner. You hung out with the coolest guy in the whole lodge." He spread his arms wide with a proud smile on his face—and almost knocked himself over. Some guy passing by with a glass of orange juice had to reach out to steady him. "Thanks, man," Christopher said, and blushed.

We looked at each other and laughed.

"Anyway, my point is, maybe your new year's resolution should be to make next year all about you," Christopher said.

"*That* sounds selfish," I said.

He grabbed a croissant from the buffet and pointed it at me. "Or is it *genius*?"

• • •

"It's such a shame we couldn't find you anything," Loretta said to me as we walked out of the third and final boutique on Main Street in downtown Evergreen. The second the biting-cold air hit my face, I felt like curling into a ball under a blanket and staying there for days.

"Loretta! Come on. You took her to all the middle-aged lady boutiques," Lauren said, then tipped her head back to watch her groaned-out breath steam toward the sky. "We need to take her to the cool stores."

"What stores are the cool stores?" Loretta asked, tugging on her leather glove. She raised one expertly plucked eyebrow in a way that was so enviable, I wanted to stop everything and beg her to teach me the secret.

"What about Tags?" Lauren said, gesturing down the street toward the bottom of the hill. "Or that new place, what's it called? I saw it last night. . . ." She tapped her leg with one hand as she thought back. "Sweets and Treats?"

"That sounds like a bakery, not a boutique," I pointed out.

"Exactly," Loretta scoffed. "And besides, no granddaughter of mine is wearing anything from that store."

She started walking up the street, her stride purposeful, making it clear that the two of us were expected to just fall in line. Lauren knocked me with her elbow to get my attention, then whispered, "I totally already went into that store."

I rolled my eyes, but laughed. We followed our grandmother, keeping a good distance so we could talk.

"Why doesn't she want us to go there?" I whispered.

"I don't know, because it's awesome," Lauren said. "We could definitely find you something cool for New Year's Eve there. Do you want to ditch her and go?"

"What? No! We can't just bail," I said, eyeing Loretta warily.

"I'm not saying we just turn around and walk away," Lauren said, leaning in, her long hair brushing my shoulder. "But I could fake sick, and then you could say you have to go home with me to keep me company or something."

"What if she comes with us?" I asked.

"We'll insist she go to this stupid dish exhibit. She's been *so* looking forward to it." Lauren grabbed my gloved hands. "Come on! Let's just do it! Live a little for once! I swear they have really nice stuff there and it's not all too short or too sexy or whatever. It's stuff even you'd like!"

I narrowed my eyes. Why did that feel like an insult? I glanced over at Loretta, who had stopped before a crosswalk and was looking at her phone. She didn't even seem to notice that her granddaughters weren't right at her sides. Maybe we could do it. Maybe . . .

"Girls!" Loretta snapped. "Don't dawdle."

"Ugh! Dang it," Lauren blurted out. And we scurried to catch up.

As we crossed the street, a huge banner across the window of the independent bookstore on the other side of Main caught my eye.

MEET POP STAR ADAM MICHEL! DECEMBER 30!

I grabbed my sister's arm, and she stopped in her tracks. "Oh my God. Oh. My. God!"

She looked where I was looking. "That's what I was trying to tell you! He's signing his new book. How crazy is that?"

"Beyond crazy." My knees were actually shaking. "I could meet Adam Michel. Like, actually talk to him."

Lauren looked me up and down. "Are you going to pee in your pants?"

I let her go. "Leave me alone. This is the biggest thing that's ever happened to me."

She shrugged. "Fair." And we kept walking. Though I actually felt light-headed. Adam Michel was coming here. For real. *The* Adam Michel. *My* Adam Michel. I seriously couldn't believe it.

The American Arts Museum was in the middle of the next block—a big white building with columns and a huge banner advertising Great American China Collections 1765–Present. Just the sight of it took the excitement right out of me. I felt like I was going to fall asleep looking at the banner. Next to me, Lauren began to cough rather convincingly. How did she get so much phlegm into her throat out of nowhere?

"Oh, girls, I'm just so excited you're finally here. I've been looking forward to sharing this exhibit with you for weeks!" Loretta said, opening the door for us. Instantly, I began to rethink the plan. Loretta was just trying to do something fun with us, and she sounded so excited. Her idea of fun pretty much sucked, but still. Her heart was in the right place. Plus the *whoosh* of warm air from the lobby was welcoming, and the inside of the museum smelled of mulled wine and spices.

Lauren stepped up the hacking. It was like she was auditioning for a role in a cough-drop commercial.

"Lauren, are you all right?" Loretta asked.

"I don't know." Lauren shot me a conspiratorial look. "My throat feels tight. I may be coming down with something."

"No. You're not. You just need some water." I grabbed my sister's arm. "I'll take her to the bathroom and we'll be right back."

I dragged Lauren away toward a sign for the restrooms, where there was also a large, modern, filtered-water fountain one could use for a quick drink or to fill up a water bottle.

"What are you doing?" Lauren asked, wrenching her arm away. "I was this close to getting us out of here."

"I don't know. I feel bad for her. She just wants to show us some dishes. How bad could it be? We'll be here for an hour, tops, and then you can take me to Sweets and whatever."

"I don't want to look at dishes!" Lauren protested, sounding very much like the younger sister in this scenario. "I want to go now!"

"Lauren, come on. Let's just—"

Lauren's phone beeped, and she checked the screen. "It's Tarek. He wants me to meet him at Starbucks."

My heart seized. "Don't even—"

But Lauren was already staggering back toward Loretta, coughing up a lung. "I'm really sorry, Loretta," she croaked. "I think I need to go lie down."

"You do look a bit clammy," Loretta said, which brought Lauren up short. I could tell she was trying very hard not to check her reflection in a window. "We'll call the driver to take you home."

"No! No, that's okay. I'll just get an Uber," Lauren said. "I do it at home all the time. You two have fun looking at dishes, and I'll see you back at the hotel."

"Nonsense. I'm not putting you in a car with a stranger. We'll call Tarek."

Loretta took out her phone and turned her back to us while she talked to the exact person who wanted to see Lauren and convinced him to come to the museum to pick her up. I scowled at my sister, and Lauren stuck her tongue out in response.

"He'll be here in five minutes," Loretta informed Lauren as she ended the call. "You should wait on the benches over by the windows where there's some sun. That should make you feel better."

"Thanks, Loretta."

Our grandmother turned to me. "Come along, Tess. I think we should start at the very beginning, don't you? Seventeen-sixty-five. Just imagine. The country wasn't even a country yet!"

"Just imagine!" Lauren said, clasping her hands in front of her.

It was all I could do not to tackle my sister to the ground. Lauren gave another cough for good measure, then slowly walked to the windows to wait for her date. I looked at Loretta. "Maybe we should go back to the hotel, too. Just in case Lauren needs us," I attempted, trying to both get out of this chore and ruin Lauren's afternoon all at once. "We can come back here another time."

Or not.

"Nonsense. Your sister is practically a grown woman, Tess. She'll be fine." Loretta offered her arm. "Besides, you should never put off until tomorrow what you can do today."

I gritted my teeth. Suddenly Christopher's suggestion about my new year's resolution came roaring back to me, filling my ears. He was right. It was about time I started doing things for myself once in a while. About time I stopped being such a people-pleaser. But my grandmother was right, too. There was no point in putting it off until New Year's Eve. I was going to start changing my life today. Right now.

Or as soon as I finished checking out two hundred fifty years' worth of famous dishware.

CHAPTER FIVE

"Daniel, hello!" Loretta greeted the front desk manager as we walked through the lobby of the Evergreen Lodge. "How is Trevor doing? Is he recovering from that flu?"

"He's doing well," Daniel replied. "And he loved the flowers you sent."

"Melissa, don't let me forget to show you that article about the new chef over at Pandalfo's," she called out to another worker. "You're going to love his story."

"I'll stop by your office after my shift," Melissa answered with a smile.

When Loretta paused to look over some paperwork from one of the decorators, I took the opportunity to slink away unnoticed. Or storm away, really. I had been holding on to pent-up anger and adrenaline for roughly two hours of boring dish viewing, and I was pretty much set to pop. I couldn't believe Lauren had abandoned me, but I was even more annoyed at myself for not speaking up and telling Loretta I wasn't interested. She was just such a force, though. It was hard to even imagine standing up to her.

But at the same time, she was somehow also one big softy. It was kind of amazing how she knew every single person who worked here by name, and also seemed to know intimate details of their lives and care about them. Even as irritated as I was about the way I'd spent my afternoon, I couldn't help feeling proud of that fact.

It wasn't Loretta's fault, I reminded myself. She hadn't done anything other than invite me along for an outing she thought I'd enjoy. I was the one who'd said yes. I was the one who'd pretended to be fascinated by scalloped edges and gold piping and hand-painted roses. I was mad at myself. Which was worse than being mad at someone else. I rounded the corner of the fireplace and found Christopher sitting in his usual spot.

"I just spent half my day listening to my grandmother postulating about the merits of bone china versus porcelain versus ceramic," I announced. "That's what I did with my afternoon."

Christopher's eyebrows rose, and he pushed himself up straighter. "Did you just use the word *postulating* in a sentence? Unironically?"

"I think I did!" I said, sitting down on the edge of the chair and putting my head in my hands, my elbows on my knees. My hair was coming loose from my ponytail in straggly chunks and I didn't care. "I'm even starting to *sound* like her."

Christopher put aside the comic book he'd been reading. It was a classic issue of *Flash*, which happened to be a show that I loved, though I'd never read the comics. Maybe I should start, and then we could compare the show to the original stories. Or would that be doing something *for* Christopher? Gah! I was losing my mind.

"Come on. There are worse things," Christopher told me. "Loretta's a cool lady."

I dropped my hands dramatically and leveled him with a disbelieving stare. "Literally no one ever has called her a cool lady."

He grinned. "Well then I'm proud to be the first." There was a carafe and four mugs on the table between us, and Christopher reached over to pour steaming hot chocolate into two of the cups. "Have some," he said. "You'll feel better."

"Do you have people bringing you treats twenty-four seven or what?" I asked.

"The staff has taken pity on me," he explained, adding marshmallows to both cups. "And I am milking that pity for all it's worth."

I was about to tell him I was too anxious for chocolate when my stomach rumbled, and I realized that I'd barely eaten anything at lunch. Loretta had insisted on a random French restaurant that had nothing recognizable on the menu. I took the cup Christopher offered and sipped. The liquid scalded my tongue, but then warmed my throat and insides. I sighed. He was right. I did feel a little better. But only a little. I took a deep breath. Then I grabbed a dozen more mini marshmallows and dumped them into the cup.

"I like your style," Christopher said, and quickly added more of the sugary blobs to his own cup.

"The thing is," I said, trying for a calmer voice, "I'm never going to get those few hours of my life back. I could have been doing something that was actually fun. Something new. Something I'd remember forever. Instead I've got something to think about to bore me to sleep when I have insomnia."

"Well, that's not nothing. If it works, you could market that." He blew on his cup.

"You're missing the point," I said.

"And what point is that?"

I clicked the back of my tongue. "The point is I'm mad as heck and I'm not gonna take it anymore."

There was a flash of excitement across Christopher's face. "What're you saying?"

I took another sip of my hot chocolate. "I'm saying, I have an idea. And it was inspired by you, really," I told him, and then blushed. Because was that the dorkiest thing ever? But Christopher just seemed intrigued.

"Go on."

"I *am* going to start doing more for myself," I said. "But it can't just be that. It can't be so general. I need to make a list. A list of things I've always wanted to do but haven't done because I've been too shy or too scared or just too . . . too . . . Tess."

"Interesting," Christopher said with a small frown. "A list?"

"Yeah, I'm a list-maker," I said, lifting my shoulders. "Totally type A and proud of it. If I make a list, I know I'll actually do the stuff on it."

"All right, then." Christopher put his cup down on the table and pulled his laptop from between the couch cushions and onto his lap. Her fired it up, stretched his fingers, cracked his knuckles, and then hovered his fingertips over the keyboard, looking at me expectantly. The mischievous glint in his eyes did melty things to my insides. "How many tasks are we putting on this list?" he asked.

"I'm thinking ten."

"Ten? For an entire year?"

"No, it's not going to be a new year's resolution," I said, scooching back in my chair and pulling my knees up under the still-warm mug in my hands. "That's the best part. It's going to be ten things I resolve to do now. *Before* New Year's. That way I'll have a solid deadline. That way I'll prove to myself I can do it—that I really can change. And I'll take that feeling into the new year."

I hadn't even really thought it through that far until I was saying it out loud, but as I heard the words coming out of my mouth, my heart swelled, and all the anxiety and anger I'd been feeling morphed into excitement. I felt like I really *needed* this. After everything that had gone on with my parents over the past few months, all the fighting and negativity and heartache, I needed something positive to take me into the new year. I needed a little bit of hope.

"Wow," Christopher said. "A list-maker who likes deadlines. You're *hard-core* type A."

I laughed mid-sip and spurted a little hot chocolate over my knees.

"That was classy," I said, grabbing a napkin to wipe up the mess. My cheeks felt flushed.

"I won't tell anyone," he assured me. He dabbed up a few droplets that had hit the table and then crumpled the napkin and tossed it at his open backpack on the floor. It landed perfectly. "Two points!"

I smiled. "And the crowd goes wild!"

Christopher grinned at me. "Okay, so. What's going to be on this list?"

He put his fingers on the keyboard again and looked me over expectantly. My shoulders slumped, and, just like that, my adrenaline oozed away.

"I have no idea."

• • •

"What about skydiving? You could go skydiving," Christopher suggested. He was sitting with both his casted leg and his healthy leg propped up on the table in front of him with pillows under his ankles and his computer on his lap, and had been taking notes diligently as we brainstormed, like my own personal assistant.

I didn't hate it, not gonna lie.

I groaned and tipped my head back over the arm of my chair, my legs dangling over the other side. "It's, like, negative ten degrees outside. No one's going skydiving," I pointed out, staring at one of the chandeliers overhead. Negative ten was kind of an exaggeration, but still. "Besides, that's not really something I've ever wanted to do."

"Afraid of heights?" he asked.

"More like afraid of death by splat," I replied, and he laughed. I picked my head up, the blood rushing back to my temples. It made me feel good, making him laugh.

"What about surfing?" he suggested.

"In the snow?"

"Snowboarding?"

"Done that," I told him.

"Skateboarding!" He snapped his fingers.

"Nope. I've skateboarded before. I used to do it all the time."

"Right. But you said you haven't since you got hurt," Christopher pointed out. "So maybe trying it again could count as a new thing."

I was touched he remembered, but I couldn't imagine trying to skateboard on the always-wet-and-icy pavement outside the resort. Besides, I had promised myself *never again* after enduring that horrible pain and spending all those weeks in a cast. Thinking about it now, though, I did wonder what life would be like if I'd never given it up. Would I still be entering competitions? Would I have, I don't know . . . gotten somewhere with it? Won trophies? Competed at Nationals? I had been pretty good at stunting. For a ten-year-old.

The sliding doors to the lobby opened, letting in a *whoosh* of cold air, as well as a large group of loud, healthy-looking twenty-somethings toting their skis and boots. I watched them until they rounded the corner toward the Alpine Bar & Grill at the far end of the airy lobby, an odd pang in my chest. Would I ever be that confident—that comfortable in my own skin? When I returned my attention to Christopher, he was watching them too—wistfully.

"It must really suck, being stuck here all day watching everyone go in and out to their activities," I said.

"It's not the *most* fun I've ever had," he said. "But I gotta say, this last hour or so has gone by pretty quickly."

"Yeah?" I said, feeling warm.

"Yeah." He lifted one shoulder. "Thanks for including me in this. It's fun."

Someone dropped their skis with a clatter, and a few people laughed and cheered. "Okay, there is one daredevil-ish thing I've never gotten up the guts to do around here," I told him.

"What?" Christopher looked intrigued.

"I've never skied one of the black diamond slopes." I bit my bottom lip, already regretting having said it out loud. Because now he was typing it into his computer. And I was *terrified* of the black diamond slopes. The one time I had skied over to the top of one of those trails, the wind had whipped up and pelted my face with a spray of ice pellets, as if the gods themselves were trying to warn me away. I had retreated to the Little Green Lodge for some soup and then taken one of the yellow trails down.

But every year since then I'd promised myself and my dad and Lauren that I was going to try, and every year I'd backed out. It was starting to get old.

"That is the perfect number nine," Christopher said.

"That's not how you broke your leg, is it? Was it on a black diamond?"

Christopher kept typing rapidly, as if he were writing the great American novel, rather than adding one item to a short list. His eyes were focused on the screen, his brow creased adorably in concentration.

"Christopher?"

"I'm trying to pretend I didn't hear you," he replied.

"Ugh! I knew it! Take it off. Forget I said anything."

I got up and made a grab for his computer, but he pulled it away, holding it up and out of my reach with his broken leg propped up between us.

"Nope! Nuh-uh! No take-backs!"

"We never said no take-backs! What is this, second grade?" I reached across his body, trying to avoid knocking into his cast, but that tipped me off-balance and I tripped. My stomach swooped and I tried to stop myself, but there was no good spot to brace my hands, and just like that, I sprawled across Christopher's lap.

Oh, God. Oh, GOD!

"Too bad you didn't put this on your list," he joked. "Because I bet you've never face-planted on a dude with a broken leg before."

Heart pounding, I carefully pushed myself away and sat down next to him on the couch. Our shoulders were touching, and my skin felt like it was on fire underneath my sweater. "Nope. Definitely never done that before. Sorry."

"It's really okay."

He put the laptop down on his other side and looked over at me, and I realized our faces were only inches apart. I could see every little line on his lips and smell the berry-licious scent of his shampoo. My pulse ticked up and then, out of nowhere, someone started singing directly into my ear.

"On the first day of Christmas, my true love gave to me a partridge in a pear tree."

Startled, I turned around and grabbed the back of the couch with both hands. There was a group of eight carolers, all decked out in ugly Christmas sweaters, busting into song in the middle of the lobby.

I locked eyes with Christopher, and we burst out laughing.

"Christmas is over!" he shouted.

"SO over!" I added.

But the carolers just kept singing jauntily, huge grins plastered on their faces.

"Ugh, how can anyone be that happy?" I grumbled, sinking down on the couch until my butt was practically dangling off the edge.

"It should be outlawed," Christopher agreed jovially, scooching down next to me.

Our shoulders pressed together again, and just like that, I couldn't stop myself from smiling.

"Look, if you must know, I didn't break my leg because of the black diamond slope," he said. "I broke my leg because I went skiing with a couple of idiot kids I barely knew, and one of them decided it would be funny to play bumper boards."

"What? Someone pushed you off the trail?" I demanded. "Who? Did you murder him?"

"Ummm . . . no. I wasn't really in the condition to take someone out right then." He chuckled. "But my parents *are* trying to get him fired."

"Wait a minute. He *works* here?" I sat up straighter, indignant. "Where does he work? Is he our age? Do you want me to talk to Loretta?"

"No! No, no, no. Honestly. My parents are all over it," he said. "And besides . . . I kind of think the whole thing is stupid. My parents are being super dramatic about it, and I wish they'd just let it go."

I blinked. "So, you don't want him fired."

"No. I mean, yeah, I guess. The guy's an asshole, seriously," he said. "And I hope I never lay eyes on the jerk again. But . . . I just don't feel the need to make a big *thing* out of it, you know?"

"But he broke your leg."

"Yeah, and it sucks. But it's not like I'm looking for revenge or something. I don't know. It's just not me."

"Wow," I said. "You are very evolved."

"Not really. I still like a good fart joke now and then."

I laughed and settled back into the couch, scooching down next to him again. We both looked at the laptop screen where the cursor blinked on the line under *9. Ski a black diamond slope.*

"Okay, only one more," Christopher said, turning his head to look at me. I could smell the sweet hot chocolate on his breath. "What's the last thing on your list going to be?"

"I don't know," I said, scanning numbers one through nine. "Why is this so hard?"

Christopher narrowed his eyes. "What about food? Is there something you've never tried that you've always wanted to try?"

Oh my God. That was it!

"Sushi!" I cried. "I've always wanted to try sushi."

"Raw fish?" Christopher shuddered, sticking out his tongue in mock disgust. "Why would anyone want to eat sushi?"

"Like, everyone in my school eats it," I told him. "But if someone asked me out to a sushi restaurant, I wouldn't even know what to order. I'd be the loser ordering chicken teriyaki or whatever."

It was my parents' fault, really. They were total meat-and-potatoes people. If we went out to dinner as a family, it was almost always to some kind of steak restaurant, or one of the Italian places near our house. Basically the only fish I'd ever had was in fish sticks.

"Put it down," I said, nodding at the computer screen. "*Eat sushi.* That's number ten."

"It's your stomach." He typed it in and hit *Save.* "And we're done. I think it's a pretty solid list, if I do say so myself."

I stared at his computer screen as the carolers launched into the *eight maids a-milking* verse. It *was* a solid list, but I thought I'd be more excited about it. For some reason I felt *meh.* Like it wasn't really real. There was something anticlimactic about this whole moment. But what did I expect? A bright light from the heavens shining down on Christopher's computer? Angels singing an aria?

Well, I did have carolers.

"So . . . when are you going to get started?"

"I feel like we need to do something," I said. "To make it official."

"Like what?" he asked. "A blood oath?"

"Um, no," I said. "Although I've never taken one of those, either."

He snorted a laugh. "What then? What makes a list more official?"

I scoured my brain until it landed on an idea. "I've got it," I said, and reached around the side of the couch for his crutches. "Let's go."

• • •

Five minutes later, the two of us were standing in the middle of Loretta's large, beautifully decorated private office, with its striped wallpaper and gleaming oak desk, watching the list print out. As soon as the paper dropped into the tray, I grabbed it and brought it over to the machine in the corner.

"What is that thing?" Christopher asked, leaning into his crutches.

"This," I said with a smile, "is Loretta's laminator. I used to play with it all the time when I was little. She let me laminate all the menus for the Easter brunch one year, and it was, like, the best day of my life."

He whistled, as if impressed. "Wow. You're a wild woman, Type A."

I grinned, kind of loving his new nickname for me. It made me want to come up with one for him, like Mr. Chill, or something, since he was so blasé about the idiot who had injured him. But Mr. Chill sounded like a super villain. I'd have to work on it.

"Hey, once you laminate something, it's sacred," I told him, firing up the machine. "You can't change a document once it's been sealed."

He tilted his head and somehow, even that small gesture, made my heart hitch. "I see your point. So, let's do it."

"Okay. Here goes nothing."

I fed the sheet of paper into the laminator. It made a soft whirring sound, and, ever so slowly, the list came out the other end with a fine, clear coating of plastic around it. Holding the still-warm document between my fingers, I inhaled the scent of fresh plastic and felt a zing of excitement all through me. Everything was going to be different from this moment on.

"One question," Christopher said. "If the list is now officially unchangeable, how are you going to check stuff off when it gets done?"

We'd purposely left space at the end of each line for a check mark so I could keep track of what I'd accomplished. Luckily, though, I'd already thought this part through. I went over to Loretta's desk and opened the top drawer. Inside was a drawer organizer, with slots for pens, pencils, paper clips, rubber bands, and Post-its. A place for everything and everything in its place. Christopher hobbled over to me and looked down. He gave an impressed whistle.

"Now I know where you get your type A from."

I picked up a permanent marker and uncapped it. "This will write on lamination, no problem," I told him.

He nodded, impressed, as I recapped the pen. "So let's get started on this thing."

"Wait . . . now?" I asked, looking up at him over the top of my all-important list. "We *just* made it official."

"Yeah, but didn't you say you wanted to get all that done before the new year?" He lifted his chin in the direction of the list, and my heart thunked into my stomach.

"Oh. Ummm . . ."

Christopher looked at his wrist, where there was no watch.
"Yeah, you've basically got less than four days."

TESS'S NEW YEAR'S BUCKET LIST

1. Make a paper airplane that actually flies
   (20 seconds at least)
2. Sing in public
3. Strike up a conversation with a stranger
4. Wear high heels outside the house
5. Make out with a guy whose last name I don't know
6. TP someone's house
7. Get Adam Michel's autograph
8. Get a short, stylish haircut
9. Ski a black diamond slope
10. Eat sushi

CHAPTER SIX

DECEMBER 28

When I woke up, the sun was shining through the slit between the heavy curtains, and I could already hear people shouting and squealing out on the ice rink. Lauren was snoring facedown into her pillow with a line of drool just beneath her mouth. For half a second, I considered snapping a photo of my perfect sister in such an imperfect state to use for later blackmail opportunities, but then I realized I was in too good of a mood.

Today I was going to get started on my list. And as soon as humanly possible. I had four days to do ten things I not only had never done, but never thought I would do. The very idea was daunting, but I was one hundred percent determined. In my entire life, I had never made a list that I didn't complete. I shoved aside the blankets and went straight for the shower. The list, in all its laminated glory, was in the center of the desk, and I gave it a little tap as I walked past it. Right next to it was Loretta's calendar of scheduled events, but luckily there wasn't anything mandatory until some pasta dinner tonight. Hopefully I'd have a couple of items checked off by then.

As the hot water streamed over my thirsty skin, I tried to wrap my brain around where to start but realized I couldn't even begin to decide without Christopher. This was as much his project as it was mine. I never would have even thought of doing it if not for him, and I had a feeling he was as excited about it as I was.

I couldn't stop thinking about the smile on his face when I'd told him my Pre–New Year's Resolution plan. Or the way he'd smelled when I'd, well, fallen on top of him. Or how close his mouth had been to mine for those few seconds on the couch.

Standing under the stream of hot water, I blushed, then giggled, and then suddenly I was just laughing like a crazy person. This was so not the way I'd ever thought this week was going to go. A few days ago, I felt like I was being exiled from home. Now I was happy—if not excited—to be here. I shut the water off and forced myself to stop giggling. It was time to get started on my day.

Unbelievably, neither the shower, nor twenty minutes of blow-drying my hair—after which it still wasn't entirely dry—woke up my sister. Neither did getting dressed or shoving all of my stuff into my backpack—for what, I wasn't sure, but I wanted to be prepared for wherever the day took me. Standing near the still-curtained window, I pulled my half-damp hair back in a bun, and a little thrill went through me at the thought of number eight on the list. If—no, *when*—I cut all my hair off, I'd never have to leave the house with wet hair again. Unless I wanted to. I snorted a laugh as I left the room, closing the door quietly behind me.

Ever since I was in eighth grade, my mother had been all over me to get a short haircut, like Emma Watson's post–Harry Potter chop, but I had always resisted. Mostly because I didn't think I was nearly pretty enough to pull it off, and partially because I was scared. Scared it would look bad. Scared of being teased. Scared people would think I *thought* I was prettier than I was.

If you don't like it, you can grow it out again, my mother always said.

But my mother wasn't the one who was going to have to live with it in the meantime. To deal with all the stares at school and people whispering, *"What was she thinking?"* But now, I felt ready. Sort of. Maybe? Being away from home was definitely part of it. I felt a little bit like a different person here. Or at least I felt like a different person from the person I was yesterday. I could only imagine the look my mom would give me when I stepped off the plane with short hair. She would probably be shocked—and disappointed I did it without her. But then my mom shouldn't have shipped me off for winter break if she wanted to be around for these things.

I took the elevator to the lobby and strode over to the couches by the fireplace to find Christopher, but Christopher wasn't there. Sitting on what I thought of as his couch were two random middle-aged parents with a pair of toddlers crawling all over them.

I must have frozen up, because they both looked at me as if maybe I was an ax murderer come to take out the whole family. It was just so weird, not seeing Christopher there. As if he lived there. Which was ridiculous. Christopher was on vacation, just like me and Lauren. Which raised the question . . . where *did* he live?

"Looking for something?" the mom asked finally. Probably she was wondering why I was standing there with my mouth hanging slightly open.

"No, I just—"

"Your buddy Christopher is in the gym," Tarek told me as he walked by, pushing a cart full of luggage. He gave me a wink, and never stopped moving.

Okay, (1) How did Tarek know Christopher? (2) How did Tarek know Christopher was my "buddy"? And (3) What the hell was Christopher doing in the gym? Didn't he know he was injured?

There was nothing for me to do but go find out.

●●●

Down the long hall and across the courtyard, I finally found the gym—a spot in the resort that I had never bothered to check out myself. I wasn't exactly an athlete, and if I did exercise, I'd do it on my bike or by going hiking with my dad—not lifting weights or doing time on an elliptical trainer. The whole place smelled like sweat and ammonia, and it made my nose wrinkle. There were only a few people inside the mirrored room, working out on treadmills and bikes, and at first I didn't see Christopher. But then I heard a set of weights clank, and I moved toward the sound. It had come from a free weight area in the back corner of the room.

What I saw there made me stop in my tracks. It made me stop breathing. Christopher was in his wheelchair, shirtless, working the biceps of his left arm with a rather large weight. At first, all I could look at were his muscles straining, the sheen of sweat across his rather cut chest. This guy couldn't be more perfect-looking if he tried. It was possible that I was developing more than a little crush. A medium-to-large–sized crush, if you will.

But then I noticed the wheelchair rocking slightly as he

moved, his cast shifting back and forth in the elevated leg rest, and I snapped out of my daze of attraction.

"What the hell are you doing?" I demanded.

He looked up, startled, and caught my eyes in the mirror. As soon as he recognized it was me, he smiled. Which, I'll admit, felt damn good.

"Good morning to you, too."

"You're going to hurt yourself."

"The doctor said it was okay as long as I only worked my arms," he said, putting the weight back on its rack. "And I've gotta stay in shape for spring ball."

I somehow held back a groan. Jocks. Couldn't live with 'em, couldn't get 'em to relax for five seconds.

"I have a surprise for you," he said.

My chest tingled, and I was momentarily distracted by the unfamiliar feeling. "You do?"

He wheeled himself over to a gym bag near the wall and plucked a sheet of green paper from inside. It was a bit crumpled, and he attempted to flatten it with his hands before holding it out to me, which only resulted in sweat stains across the black print.

"Fifteenth Annual Evergreen Lodge Holiday Karaoke Party," I read. The words *Sing in Public* swam across my mind's eye. Why had I agreed to do any of this, again?

"It's tonight in the Pinecone Lounge. What're the chances?" Christopher said. "You have about ten hours to figure out what you're going to sing." He took out a white towel and wiped the sweat from his brow. "And I figured you could wear heels while you do it. Kill two birds with one stone."

Wow. He'd really put a lot of thought into this. I was flattered.

But putting aside the sheer terror I felt at the very idea of singing in public, let alone the cluelessness over what song would embarrass me the least, there was still just one problem.

"Ummm . . . I don't actually own a pair of heels."

"You don't?" He glanced down at my feet, as if a pair of heels would suddenly appear on them. Unfortunately, I was wearing my favorite pair of high-top Converse. Just about as far away from Louboutins as you could get.

"If I did, don't you think I would have worn them by now, thereby precluding me from putting *Wear high heels* on my list?" I snapped the list out of my backpack and held it up.

Christopher laughed. "All right, don't take my head off, Type A. It was an innocent question."

"I'm five foot ten," I tell him. "High heels always seemed . . . I don't know . . . unnecessary. And the one time my mom made me try them on for my cousin's wedding, I felt like a freak show. I had to beg her to let me wear flats until she finally relented."

"Wait. You're five ten?" he asked, blanching slightly as he gazed up at me.

"Yeah, why?" I looked him up and down, realizing I'd never actually seen him standing up straight. Since we'd met, he'd either been sitting on a couch, sitting in a wheelchair, or hunched over crutches. "How tall are you?"

"Oh, um . . . I don't really pay attention to that stuff."

"Yeah, right. A basketball player who doesn't know how tall he is? Why do I not believe that?" I joked.

"Whatever. Let's just figure out this heel problem," he said, shoving his towel back in his bag and pulling out a T-shirt. I let it die, because clearly it was a sore subject, but now I couldn't help trying to size him up with my eyes. When he glanced up at me again, it was with a shrewd gaze, as if he knew what I was doing, so I quickly looked away.

"Maybe you can borrow a pair from your sister?" he suggested.

I shook my head. "Lauren's feet are two sizes smaller than mine," I told him, trying not to be self-conscious about it. "I'm going to need to go shopping."

"I guess we could go into town. We have plenty of time," Christopher said. "Do you drive?"

"We can't get our license in Pennsylvania until we're seventeen," I said. "I just got my permit in October."

"Where're you from in Pennsylvania?" he asked, sounding intrigued.

"Philly. Why? Where do you live?"

"Princeton," he replied. "So, not that far from you." We smiled at each other, and my skin warmed. Was he implying that he wouldn't mind seeing me once this ridiculous trip was over and we were both back home? Suddenly I was imagining introducing him to my friends. Taking him to the prom. Making everyone I'd ever met swoon with jealousy.

Okay, Tess. Chill.

"What about Lauren?" he asked.

"Yep. She can drive." I pulled out my phone and started a text, glad to have an excuse to stop fantasizing. "And luckily, she'll take pretty much any excuse to go shopping."

• • •

Christopher went back to his room to wrap his cast in plastic and take a shower, while I went in search of my dear sister. She was no longer in our room, having left her bedsheets in a tangle and four separate, very wet towels on the floor of the bathroom. Who the heck needed four towels? And was she really unaware that there were two empty towel bars right there for her use? I carefully hung up the damp towels and let the door lock behind me. After checking the restaurant and the gift shop, I was hit with the strong scent of fresh coffee and rolled my eyes. Right. The Best Bean Café. I'd almost spaced on Lauren's caffeine addiction.

Sure enough, I found my sister sitting at the window counter in the sun, her sunglasses on, her hair perfectly blow-dried, looking utterly glam as she sipped a latte and flipped through some kind of feed on her phone. A pair of college-aged guys at the counter were blatantly checking her out and kept nudging each other and laughing. I shot them a withering look, which neither seemed to notice as I stepped over to the register.

"Good morning!" The guy behind the counter was about my age with a healthy tan and long brown hair he wore back in a low ponytail. He was wearing one of the green Evergreen Lodge polo shirts with a Best Bean Café apron over it. His smile was like something out of a toothpaste commercial. "What can I get for ya?"

"Can I have a latte, please?" I asked, keeping one eye on my sister to make sure she didn't get away.

"Coming right up. Name?"

"Tess," I said, and he wrote it on a paper cup.

"Great name! Like *Tess of the D'Urbervilles*," he told me. "I'm Damon."

"Have you read *Tess of the D'Urbervilles*?" I asked, surprised.

"I tried. Bored the crap outta me, though."

I laughed. "Well, at least you tried."

"Thanks. Your order will be up in a minute at the pickup counter." He gestured in that direction. "Nice to meet you, Tess."

"You too," I said warmly, feeling kind of proud of myself for not getting tongue-tangled in front of a cute boy.

I grabbed my coffee, added some sugar, and then walked over and slid onto the stool next to Lauren's.

"Good morning!"

"Ugh. Do you have to be so loud?" Lauren grumbled, taking a sip of her coffee.

"I'm not being loud. I'm speaking at a perfectly normal volume."

Lauren pressed her lips together. "Normal to you."

Oooookay. Someone wasn't in the best mood. "Did you not sleep well?" I asked, tossing my backpack under the chair and taking a sip of my drink.

"I was up late texting with Tarek." Only when she said Tarek's name did a wisp of a smile appear on her face.

"Oh. That's cool." It looked like I wasn't the only one with a medium-to-large-sized crush. "He seems nice," I said, buttering her up. Always the best policy if I was about to ask for a favor.

"He is. Very." Lauren looked out the window, and I couldn't tell if she was thinking about Tarek or trying to be mysterious and aloof in order to appear cooler. It was weird how I could live with my sister my whole life and still not get her at all sometimes.

"He's in college, you know. He goes to Bennington." She sipped her coffee again. "He's just working here over break, and he said he's hoping to travel this summer. How cool is that? We could potentially go to Europe together."

Unbelievable. Only my sister could work someone she met two

days ago into her summer plans and think it was realistic. But then again, I was just thinking about looking up the train schedules between Philadelphia and Princeton, so who was I to judge?

"So, what're you doing today?" I swung my legs back and forth under my stool, feeling a mix of excitement, adrenaline, and total dread that my sister was going to turn me down cold. A solid prediction, since Lauren was now eyeing me skeptically over the top of her sunglasses.

"Whatever Loretta tells me to, I thought. She already texted me to see if I felt any better and ask if I'd taken my temperature, so I had to deal with that debacle. I told her it was a false alarm and I felt way better after a good night's sleep. Old people *love* a good night's sleep." She rolled her eyes. "Why? What did you have in mind?"

"There's nothing on Loretta's schedule until tonight. I double-checked."

"Why am I not surprised?" She sat up straight, stretched, then leaned back against the counter behind her, all casual. "So, spill, little sis. What's up?"

"I need you to drive me into town." I held my breath.

She didn't blink. "In what car?"

"We could borrow one from the resort. They have all those cars for taking people to parties off property and stuff. I'm sure Loretta would let us take one."

Lauren pushed her sunglasses back up with the tip of her middle finger. "Do you even hear yourself? Loretta's not letting us do anything other than what's on her schedule. If you want to take a car, we're going to have to 'borrow' one with the help of some kindly member of the staff." She threw air quotes around the word *borrow*.

"Okay, fine," I said. "We'll do that."

"Wait a minute, wait a minute." Lauren threw up her palms. "That would be breaking the rules, Tess. You do realize that, right?"

My face burned. "God, Lauren, can you give me a break? It's not like I *always* follow the rules."

"Name me one time you didn't," Lauren said.

"Oh, I don't know . . . maybe fifth grade when I snuck out to that skateboarding competition Mom forbid me to compete in and broke my freaking ankle?"

Lauren scoffed. She *scoffed.* My cheeks burned in indignation. "I'm sorry, but you can't keep going back to that well for the rest of your life. It was six years ago! And it wasn't even that bad!"

"I was in the hospital for an entire day!"

"I meant that the sneaking out wasn't that bad, not that the injury wasn't that bad," Lauren said. She slid her phone into her pocket and picked up her coffee, getting ready to leave.

"Fine, if I'm so lame then help a girl out. Help me break the rules. Let's 'borrow' a car and go into town." I stood up and picked up my bag. "I bet Tarek would help us. You could talk him into it no problem."

Lauren hung her head back dramatically for half a second, but then turned to face me. "First of all, obviously I can talk him into it no problem. Second of all . . . why do you need to go into town?"

"I need a new pair of shoes." I took a deep breath. "I want you to help me buy a pair of heels."

I mumbled the last few words, but that didn't stop Lauren's face from completely lighting up. "No. Freaking. Way!"

"It's not that big a deal," I said under my breath.

"Are you kidding? This is a *huge* deal!" she cried loudly. "My baby sister's all grown up!"

A few people at nearby café tables turned to look at us, some of them amused, others obviously feeling my pain.

"Shhhh!" I hissed. Damon was walking by, without his apron now, clearly having finished his shift. He shot me a pitying glance, but was also trying not to laugh. "You're embarrassing me." My phone vibrated in my hand. A text from Christopher.

Ready to go. In lobby. Where are you guys?

I quickly texted back.

Best Bean

"I don't know, T," Lauren said, glancing at her wrist, even though she never wore a watch. "I have some serious Netflix binging to do. What's in it for me?"

I hesitated, at a loss. Did my sister expect me to bribe her? Offer to buy her a pair of shoes, too? It wasn't like I was rolling in money. All I had on me was the cash my Nana and Papi had given me for Christmas. My mother refused to let me get a real job until I got my driver's license, and I'd spent all my liquid funds on Christmas gifts. Lauren, meanwhile, had been working at Ultimate Beauty for the last year and socking away every paycheck for her European adventure. She'd given all of us handmade cards for Christmas. Which was nice, I guess, but still.

"I—"

"Hey, Type A! There you are!"

Lauren turned around at the sound of Christopher's voice. She pushed her sunglasses up into her hair—for a better look, I could only imagine. He made his way over to us on his crutches, deftly avoiding the small tables and chairs, and paused next to Lauren.

"Let me just grab some coffee. I could go for one after that workout." He looked at my sister and held out a hand, clamping his crutch under his arm. "Hey. I'm Christopher," he said.

Lauren smiled and shook his hand. "I'm—"

"The evil sister, I know."

I snorted, then slapped my free hand over my mouth. Lauren's jaw dropped, and she shot me a *WTH* look.

"Christopher is coming with us," I told her.

"This guy?" Lauren pointed across her body at Christopher, her eyes on me. "The one who just called me evil?"

"Well, you are a little evil," I joked.

Lauren smirked.

"Yeah, and we're gonna need a van, probably," Christopher pointed out. "So I can prop up my leg."

Lauren's eyes trailed from his sock-covered foot, sticking out of his cast, all the way up his body to his green, green eyes.

"Okay, *fine*," she said. "But by the end of the day, you'd better take back that evil comment." She put her sunglasses back on and pointed at me. "You get him his coffee and meet me in the garage in ten minutes. By the time you get there, I'll have a van for us."

She turned and flounced away, leaving me shaking my head. I should have mentioned Christopher from the very beginning. The fastest way to my sister's heart was with a hot guy.

CHAPTER SEVEN

Downtown Evergreen was like something out of a dusty classic picture book featuring stories from a simpler time. Main street was a wide, two-lane road lined with flowerpots (currently holding decorated evergreen shrubs) and old-fashioned lampposts, each of these hung with a ball of holly and festooned with red ribbon. Colorful awnings adorned the mom-and-pop shops, which included an actual five-and-dime store, a stationery store called Write or Wrong, and a barbershop with the classic swirling striped barbershop pole. There was a Starbucks, and a couple of banks, but otherwise, it was as if time had stopped, and everyone who lived and worked there meant to keep it that way. The plate-glass windows shone, the wrought-iron trellises were freshly painted, and there wasn't a stray bit of garbage anywhere. The only speck of anything on the sidewalks was the leftover salt from when the store owners had dealt with the ice that morning.

"Where is this place, anyway?" I asked, following my sister up the hill, past where most of the shops lived. I kept looking back at Christopher, who was bringing up the rear, gamely navigating around other pedestrians with his crutches. The place was so jammed, Lauren had been forced to park in a municipal lot a couple of blocks outside of town, but Christopher hadn't complained once.

"It's in an old Victorian house up here. It's so cool. Wait until you see."

Lauren actually seemed excited. Maybe the way to my sister's heart was actually through shopping. Could it be that there was more than one? Maybe I should stop waiting for my sister to stop treating me like crap and start offering to do the things she liked to do. This was, at least, more pleasant than most of the time we'd spent together lately. Although, it wasn't like she ever offered to hang out with me at the bookstore or had come to one of the plays I worked on without being bribed by a parent.

"We're here," Lauren announced finally, slightly out of breath. She clomped up the steps of the small home, which were painted a light lavender, and opened the door with a flourish.

I looked up. The words SWEETS AND TREATS were painted on the front window of the pretty, gingerbread-style house. In the window display, shoes, purses, and jewelry were positioned on little glittering ski slopes, as if they were taking morning runs. "Isn't this the place Loretta basically forbid us to go?"

Lauren rolled her eyes, and I flinched, waiting for the put-down that I knew, from experience, was on the tip of her tongue. But then Christopher arrived behind me—I could smell the fruity scent of his shampoo—and Lauren stopped herself. Clearly she didn't want to look like a jerk in front of him. Hanging out with Christopher was turning out to have so many benefits.

"Come on," Lauren said. "They have the cutest stuff. Unless you want to buy a pair of sensible pumps from one of the middle-aged-lady stores downtown."

"You definitely don't want to do that," Christopher offered, eyes twinkling.

I went up the stairs and held the door for Christopher, who made his way ever so slowly toward us. He winced with each step, and I started to feel very guilty about this whole endeavor. But then, he was the one who'd insisted on coming along. Almost as if he wanted to spend time with me and would endure anything to do it.

My heart did a little pitter-patter dance at the thought.

"You'd think they'd be required to install a ramp," he muttered under his breath as he finally arrived, a sheen of sweat across his forehead. "Isn't that, like, a law?"

"Are you all right?" I asked. "We don't have to do this. I feel like you should be home in bed."

"Probably." He gave me a heart-stopping grin. "But why the heck would I want to do that when I'm about to watch you try on shoes?"

The weird thing was, it was clear he really meant it.

. . .

Half an hour and about twenty pairs of painful shoes later, I was about ready to give up. Why? Why did high-heeled shoes exist? And why did anyone want to wear them—ever? My calves ached and my toes were pinched and there was a blister forming on the back of one of my heels. And this was just from *trying them on.* I honestly couldn't believe Loretta walked around in shoes like this all day. Were her feet made of steel?

Lauren was texting on her phone, and Ainsley—the salesperson who had been gamely running up and down the stairs to the stockroom for new pairs—looked desperate as I kicked off the latest pair—strappy torture devices covered in silver glitter. Honestly, it felt as if someone had taken a hacksaw to the tops of my feet.

"I think you've tried on every pair that's lower than three inches," Ainsley said, biting her bottom lip, which was painted a deep shade of purple and outlined in black. "If you were willing to go a bit higher, I could—"

"No. She can't handle higher," Lauren said, shoving her phone away. "Trust me on this. You ever seen a baby giraffe video?"

Ainsley's plucked eyebrows rose. "Oh, really?" she said, and scrunched up her face. "That bad?"

"That bad," Lauren confirmed.

"Hey, I am *not* a baby giraffe," I grumbled, and they both looked at me hopefully. "But I really don't want to go above two inches," I said with an apologetic shrug. Honestly, if I'd only tried on two-inch pairs so far, I was pretty sure three inches would actually kill me.

"I'm sorry," Ainsley said. "I really don't have anything else I can show you."

Lauren tipped her head back and groaned.

"Wait! What about these? Do these count?" Christopher came out from behind one of the shelves with a boot in his hand. It was a tall brown boot with a fairly slim, but not ridiculously slim, high heel.

"Count for what?" Lauren asked. "Why are we even doing this again?"

I had somehow found a way to get through the last hour without mentioning the list to my sister. Now she and Ainsley were eyeing me with interest, as if I was about to make some sort of deep confession. I didn't care what they thought they were waiting for, though. I locked eyes with Christopher. He lifted one shoulder, saying it was up to me. And it *was* up to me, wasn't it? It was my list. My idea. My goals. I could decide what counted as "high heels" and what didn't.

"Yes, those do count," I said. Partially because I was sick of this whole exercise already and partially because the boots looked like something I might actually wear again—as long as they didn't do further damage to my already pissed-off feet. They were a very lush shade of tannish-brown, and they looked soft.

"I'll get them in your size!" Ainsley announced, hoofing it for the stairs once again. "I'm totally skipping the gym after this."

Lauren laughed. "Do you remember that time Mom took us shopping for back-to-school shoes, and the saleswoman told her I had fat feet?"

"What?" I cried. "No way."

Christopher tilted his head, trying to get a look at Lauren's feet, but she made a show of tucking them under her chair. I kind of couldn't believe that Lauren would have said anything unflattering about herself in front of a guy.

"You don't remember that?" Lauren picked up a bracelet from a table next to her chair and tried it on. The rhinestones flashed in the sunlight, streaming through the tall windows across the way. "I burst into tears and threw a fit."

"Really?" I had zero recollection of this event. "How old were we?"

Lauren narrowed her eyes and added another bracelet. "I think I was seven, so you were five."

"What did mom do?"

"She went into this whole lecture about how the woman was trying to indoctrinate her girls into societal norms of beauty and weight and she should be ashamed of herself."

"Yeah, that sounds like mom," I said with a laugh. Then I remembered I was mad at my mother, and I felt a sour sort of burning around my heart. "I can't believe you remember that."

"I was so psyched that when I got home, I wrote it down. What I could spell of it, anyway." She sighed, took off the bracelets, and put them back on the table. "Our mom's the coolest," she told Christopher.

"Sounds like it," he replied. "I'm bummed I don't get to meet her."

"Whatever. It's not *that* big a loss," I muttered.

Lauren turned, as if she was about to ask me what I meant by that, when Ainsley came barreling down the stairs. "Got 'em! Size ten!"

She strode over to me and opened the forest green box, then removed all the plastic and paper from inside the tall shaft of the boots. I sat down and held my breath as I carefully pushed my right foot into the first boot. If these didn't work, I had no idea what I was going to do. Other than go buy a pair of middle-aged-lady pumps from a store downtown. I zipped up the boot.

"How does it feel?" Ainsley asked.

"So far so good," I replied, wriggling my toes. I was relieved to discover they could actually move. Meanwhile, it seemed like every-one around me was crossing their fingers and toes. Possibly even the woman behind the register over in the corner, who'd been helping every other customer who came in while Ainsley dealt with me.

I zipped up the other boot and stood. There was the tiniest wobble, but then I straightened and realized I felt almost solid. It was still weird, being a whole two inches taller, but I didn't feel quite so . . . not me as I had in all the hard, toeless, patent heels I'd tried on before.

"Do the walk," Lauren instructed.

I walked down the length of the throw rug that encompassed the shoe area of the store, then back again. Nothing hurt. Well, aside from that heel blister, which had been throbbing even before I'd put on the boots. I paused at the far end, then pivoted to look back at three expectant faces. Excitement bubbled up inside my chest.

"They're good!" I declared.

"Woo-hoo!" Ainsley cheered.

Then Lauren's phone rang. She looked at it and grimaced. "It's Loretta."

My heart thunked. Were we caught? Lauren picked up.

"Hey, Loretta! How's—"

I heard Loretta's angry voice shouting through the phone and I looked at Christopher, who had blanched.

Yep. We were definitely caught.

• • •

"She was annoyed because we missed some kind of family portrait day or something," Lauren said as she drove the van at top speed back toward the resort. "I thought you said you double-checked the schedule."

In the back seat, Christopher braced himself against the wall at his side and the seat back behind him. In my lap, I held the red plaid paper bag with my new boots inside. In the end, I hadn't had to buy Lauren her own pair of shoes, but I had gotten Ainsley to throw in one of the bracelets my sister was admiring. It was the least I could do.

Now, I had to grit my teeth against my nerves. "I did double-check. I saw nothing about family portraits. And could you try to not kill my friend back there?"

Lauren shot me a mischievous side-eye. "Friend?" she whispered. "Or more than friend?"

"Shhh!" I blushed.

"Ooooooh!" Lauren teased. "I knew it!"

"Knew what?" Christopher called out.

"Nothing!" both Lauren and I responded, Lauren in a singsong and me in a strained wail.

"No fair keeping secrets from the dude in the back!" Christopher shouted, and Lauren and I laughed. It felt good to laugh with my sister. Better than I would have ever admitted.

"Anyway, she wants us to go to some Frank Sinatra dinner to make up for it." Lauren gave a massive eye roll. "It's, like, all the pasta you can eat and some old dude singing some dead dude's songs."

"*That* I remember seeing on the schedule," I said.

"Sinatra and Pasta!" Christopher shouted. "It's actually a pretty fun time. We go every year."

"I'm not so sure about this *friend* of yours," Lauren said quietly. "He has questionable taste."

"Hey! I picked out the boots!" Christopher pointed out.

"You heard that?" Lauren demanded.

Crap. Did that mean he'd also heard the "more than friend" comment?

"Lauren, I can't go to dinner tonight. You have to cover for me."

Lauren was so shocked she almost drove off the road. "Wait a minute, what? Did we just drive through some sort of wormhole? Tess wants *me* to cover for *her*?"

"Oh my God! Can we not make a big deal out of this?" I demanded, glancing back at Christopher.

"It's actually fine," he assured me. "Sinatra and Pasta is at, like, six p.m. The karaoke party doesn't start until nine. You can do both."

"The karaoke party? That's what you want me to cover for?" Lauren was clearly thrown. "But you don't sing."

"I do now," I said, determined. Up ahead, the sign for Evergreen Lodge, shaped like—what else—a forest of evergreen trees, loomed. "Tonight, I wear heels and sing karaoke."

Lauren took the turn so fast, the van's tires squealed. "Oh yeah. Definitely a wormhole," she said.

CHAPTER EIGHT

It was the longest afternoon of my life. Loretta insisted that we sit down for lunch with her, and then spent the entire meal grilling us about school and grades and friends and "significant others" until I felt like I'd been turned inside out. Lauren seemed to be taking it even worse, what with the third degree about this "ill-advised year off" she was planning to take. Loretta told her that if she insisted on backpacking through Europe, Loretta could at least provide her with a list of hotels where she could pick up "respectable" jobs along the way and "do something useful with her time."

"I have a lot of friends in this business," Loretta told her, touching her napkin to her lips, which were somehow still perfectly outlined and lipsticked. "We boutique hotel owners like to support one another."

"Oh, Dad already gave me a list of contacts at all the Galileo hotels, just in case," Lauren said with a confident smile. We both looked at Loretta, sure that this would appease her. But Loretta, instead, went very still.

One thing no one in my family ever talked about was the fact that my father had left Evergreen Lodge behind for a prestigious job at the international Galileo hotel chain. In his position as legal counsel for Galileo, he got to travel all over the world, which he never would have been able to do working for Loretta. But sometimes, like right then, it was pretty clear that Loretta wasn't happy about it. Me and my mom; Dad and Loretta. Our relationships were definitely complicated.

"Fine," Loretta said finally. "That's that, then."

Lauren and I exchanged a look, unsure of what to do next.

And then Loretta recovered and launched into all the ways that Lauren could get lost or assaulted or murdered and told her that she'd better pack pepper spray. By the end of the lecture, Lauren was holding a fork like a shiv and looked like she wouldn't mind committing murder. Or maybe stabbing herself in the ear so she wouldn't have to hear any more.

Mercifully, once we were done eating, Loretta let us go. She had meetings all afternoon and told us we could have some time to ourselves, provided we meet her for the Sinatra and Pasta dinner at 6 p.m. sharp. Lauren shot out of her chair like it was equipped with an ejector seat, and I went right back to our room to practice walking around in my new boots.

That had lasted all of about ten minutes. Then I'd opened up my laptop to look up the details of the Adam Michel signing in town on New Year's Eve. I had heard about Adam's autobiography ages ago on his Instagram, but hadn't realized it was coming out this month. What were the chances that my favorite singer of all time was signing his book at the rinky-dink bookstore in Nowheresville, Vermont, on the exact week that I was here? It was like fate, and I couldn't let the opportunity pass me by.

The signing started at noon, but there was no end time listed.

People were probably going to be lining up for hours beforehand, but how many books would he sign? How long would he stay to meet and greet his fans? I couldn't imagine there were thousands of Adam Michel fans hanging out in Evergreen right now, but what did I know? Maybe people had traveled here for this once-in-a-lifetime opportunity. Maybe there were people staying at this very hotel whose only purpose for being here was meeting Adam Michel. If I was going to check this one off my list, I'd have to get there early.

And I was totally going to have to plan out what to say beforehand, so that I wouldn't just turn into an incoherent puddle of goo.

Once I'd made a note of the details on the bookstore website and closed my laptop, I was instantly bored. I had nothing to do. I could have read some more of *Sense and Sensibility*, of course, but there was no way I'd be able to concentrate right now. In just a few hours, I was going to be singing in front of dozens of people. In heels. And I hadn't even picked out a song.

Would it be dozens of people? What if it was hundreds? What if the entire resort came to this thing? And people from town? And people from *other* towns? What if all the Adam Michel fans staying at the lodge showed up? How popular was this karaoke thing, anyway?

I looked around the room, my nerves forming a tangled web in my stomach. I had to find something to do. I couldn't just sit around here all afternoon and freak myself out.

I located the remote under a pile of Lauren's clothes and turned on the TV, but a quick flip through the hundred or so channels revealed there was nothing on worth watching. There was always streaming, but I couldn't think of a single show I was dying to see. Grunting in frustration, I turned off the TV again and tossed the remote on my bed. The silence was deafening. I glanced at the clock. Only a half hour had passed since I'd escaped from that awful lunch.

"What the hell am I supposed to do for the next three hours?" I said aloud.

I knew I should decide on a song to sing. Maybe . . . practice? The very idea tied my chest in knots and made me feel silly. Suddenly the room felt way too small. I grabbed my phone and walked out into the empty hallway, my heart pounding so erratically it was like a wild thing with a mind of its own. Leaning back against the wall in the cool hallway, I texted Christopher.

> **Where are you?**
> In my room. What's up?
> **What room#?**
> 115
> **Can I come down?**
> Sure. Everything OK?
> **I think I'm having a heart attack.**
> Come now

I found my way to the elevators and hit the button for the first floor, then pushed myself back against the rear of the cubicle with my hands behind me and tried to breathe. It didn't help that the piped-in music was a fairly psychotic rendition of "Carol of the Bells." Repetitive, annoying, and shrill. The second the door opened, I flung myself into the hall and turned left. Christopher was standing at the door of his room, waiting for me.

"Hi!" he said brightly. But as I got closer, his face slowly fell. "You look like you're gonna barf."

"I might," I said, pressing my phone between my palms. "Why did I decide to do this? I can't sing in public. I can't. It's ridiculous. I can't even do oral book reports. What made me think I could—"

"Okay, okay, calm down." Keeping his crutches clamped under his arms, Christopher reached out and placed his two large, warm, hands on my shoulders. Every inch of me responded. Suddenly all I wanted to do in the world was sink against his chest and let him hug me. What would that even feel like? It was an acute sort of longing I'd never experienced before in my life, and now I was even tenser. Like, if I didn't get him to hug me, I'd explode. "Take a deep breath," Christopher said calmly.

I did. My lungs clenched.

"Now let it out!" he said, giving me the slightest shake. I blew it out through pursed lips, turning my head slightly sideways just in case my breath was bad. But then I kind of started to hyper-ventilate.

"Oh God. I think I've forgotten how to breathe!" I wailed.

"Right. What you need is a distraction. Something to do until it's time to go to the dinner," Christopher suggested. "We can't have you not breathing for the next two hours."

"Okay, but I tried that. Nothing worked."

Christopher smiled. "Did you try paper airplanes?"

· · ·

First, we had to find paper, which was harder than it sounded in a hotel where most people used text or email to communicate, and the gift shop had only small, gifty, journal-style notebooks. In the end, I wound up raiding my grandmother's office again—luckily she was out at "a meeting with the legal team," according to her assistant, Frank—and stealing a ream of printer paper. I brought it back to Christopher's room, where he was propped up on his bed with his cast laid out in front of him and his laptop on his lap. He'd given me his spare key, so I was able to just walk in, and my heart caught a bit when I saw him there, his T-shirt pulled taut across his chest.

"What're you doing?" I asked.

"Research."

He smiled and turned the computer around. On the screen, a pair of hands expertly folded a standard piece of bright blue paper into an airplane that looked like something out of an air force textbook.

"Oh, cool. Now I wish I had something better than white." I held up the package of paper dejectedly.

"Don't worry. I don't think it's the color that makes it fly far," Christopher joked. "Here. Sit so we can watch this together."

Okay. Sure. Sit with him on his bed. That was something I could totally do and not be awkward about it at all.

"Where are your parents?" I asked casually, while simultaneously imagining them walking in to find a strange girl on their son's bed with him and freaking out.

"Oh, I have my own room," he said. "Also they had to go to a meeting. We're not meeting up until dinner."

"A meeting?" I asked.

His face reddened slightly. "It's a long story. Even when we're on vacation, my parents somehow find ways to attend meetings. They're chill like that."

Not that he was bitter or anything. I couldn't blame him, though. My dad did travel for work a lot, but when we went on vacation together, he was always super focused on us—on making family time family time. Sometimes it was actually a little much. But seeing the look on Christopher's face now made me glad my father was always so involved. At least I never felt ignored.

"You okay over there?"

It wasn't until Christopher spoke that I realized I'd sort of frozen in place and was hovering next to his bed awkwardly.

"Fine," I said, swiping my ponytail over my shoulder, all casual-like. I dropped the paper on the desk and walked around to sit down on the opposite side of the bed, my pulse racing. Christopher and I were entirely alone, in his private room, with the door locked and the shades half-drawn. And yep. I was about to crawl into bed with him.

Well, not exactly, I told myself. The bed was completely made. And all we were doing was sitting there to watch YouTube instructional videos. I had to think of it like it was a couch. And Christopher was just a friend. And we'd been assigned by old, smelly Mr. Walton back home to work on a physics project together. No big deal.

So, I sat. Well, perched, really, my feet still on the floor. Which meant I had to twist uncomfortably to face the computer.

"Can you even see from over there?" he asked.

I laughed. "Um, no." It was a king-size bed. I was basically three feet away from him. I swung my legs up onto the bed and scooched over until we were so close our shoulders touched. His skin was *so* warm, even through the fabric of our shirts, and my face lit up like one of the Christmas trees in the lobby. I forced myself to stay still. To concentrate. To really listen to what the guy on the computer was saying about precise folds and even wings.

"This doesn't look that hard," Christopher said finally. "We can totally do this."

Was he kidding? These paper airplanes were like tiny works of art. I remembered going to an origami party once in middle school and ending up in tears because I couldn't get my corners precise enough. Type A me couldn't handle not being good at something that required precision.

"Totally," I echoed, lying through my teeth. "But where are we going to fly them from? He says finding a high throwing point is key."

"We could go outside, I guess," Christopher said. "Use one of the decks or balconies?"

I looked past him out the window, where the tops of the evergreen trees swayed.

"It's too windy," I pointed out.

"Okay, but if the wind catches it, it'll fly *really* far," he countered.

I gave him an admonishing look. "That feels like cheating."

"Well, your family owns this place, right?" Christopher said, setting the computer aside and turning to look at me. I tried not to be distracted by the fact that he was so close. That his breath smelled like peppermint. That we were on a bed, and he was very ill-equipped to run away. "I mean, yeah, my family comes here every Christmas, but you must still know it better than I do. Is there anywhere indoors that we could use as a launching pad?"

I tore my gaze away from his lips and closed my eyes, thinking. There was the restaurant and the ballrooms and the kitchen, the gym and the spa and . . .

Then, it hit me. "I've got just the place."

• • •

Around the indoor pool there were two floors of open hallways overlooking the water. Guest rooms lined the far side of the hall, but the inside was made up of a half wall so guests could look over and see people swimming. Christopher and I set up our launching spot just outside the elevators on the third floor. Overhead, the ceiling was made up of skylights, lending a killer view of the bright blue sky, with wispy clouds chasing one another from pane to pane. Down below, about two dozen people lounged in cushy chairs, reading magazines and books or playing on their phones, while a whole gaggle of kids splashed and screamed in the crystal clear water.

"This is perfect," Christopher said, glancing over the barrier. "Let's do it."

"I don't know. I didn't expect there to be so many people down there," I said, chewing the inside of my cheek. "I don't want to bother anybody."

"I can take care of that." Before I had even registered what he'd said, he whistled loudly, and the noise rising up from around the pool all but stopped.

"What're you doing?" I whispered, smacking his arm with the back of my hand.

"Okay, we need to work on this hitting problem you have," he said quietly. "Unless it means you like me, in which case, I'm cool with it."

I blushed like crazy. Oh my God, he was right. Isn't that what they always said? That if kids pushed each other around on the playground, it meant they were crushing on each other? Ugh, could I be more obvious? I clasped my hands behind me and promised myself I'd have better control.

Christopher, however, just smiled. "Hi, everyone!" he called out to the people down below, waving like a princess on a parade float. "My name's Christopher, and this is Tess. Wave to the people, Tess," he directed.

I managed a meek wave, resolving to murder Christopher for this later.

"We're going to do a little science experiment that involves paper planes, so if you see anything fluttering toward you, you're not under attack, it's just paper. Cool?"

For a long moment there was no response, and then some little kid called up, "If we catch them, can we keep them?"

Christopher shrugged. "Sure. Knock yourself out."

"Cool!" The kid and some others cheered, and then Christopher turned to grin at me. "Problem solved."

"You're crazy," I told him, pulling the first paper airplane out of the backpack where we'd stashed them.

"You're not the first person who's told me that."

I wondered who else had called him out for his shenanigans in the past. It was weird, knowing that he had a whole life somewhere other than here. That he had friends and maybe even a girlfriend, and a bedroom and a school and a basketball team. All of which he'd be going back to in a few days when I went back to Philly. Maybe that was part of the charm of meeting someone on vacation. It felt as if they'd been created just for you. But it wasn't true. And for a moment, I felt weirdly depressed. And jealous of all the people in Princeton, NJ.

"Tess?" he prompted.

I shook myself out of it. We were on a mission here.

"Get the timer ready," I instructed.

Christopher pulled out his phone and opened the timer. I

readied the airplane and he counted me down. "Okay. Three, two, one. Let 'er rip!"

I tossed the airplane, slightly up and as straight as possible, just as the instructional video had recommended. But I knew it was wrong the second the plane left my fingers. The paper shot up for half a second, then took a nosedive and plummeted, spiraling toward the pool. It hit the water, and a kid in a SpongeBob SquarePants bathing suit shrieked and flung himself toward it.

"Yeah, that didn't work," I said.

"Nope. Five and a half seconds." Christopher held up his phone to confirm.

I clucked my tongue. "What'd I do wrong?"

"Maybe it wasn't you. Maybe it was the plane," he suggested. "It could have been too front-heavy. Try one of those little short ones."

I carefully dug through the pile of planes until I found what he was looking for. It was a squat little plane that seemed a bit front-heavy to me as well, half the page having been folded into the upper half. But the guy on YouTube had said it was guaranteed to fly the farthest, so who was I to argue? YouTubers knew everything, right?

"Give it a try," Christopher said.

I chucked the little plane. He hit the timer. And the plane dropped like a stone onto the head of a mom almost directly below where we were standing.

"Sorry!" I called out, mortified.

The woman waved up at us, carefree, and turned the page in her book, folding the airplane into it to use as a bookmark. No harm, no foul.

"This isn't working," I grumbled, still embarrassed.

"It's okay!" Christopher chided me. "We have like ten more to try. Don't give up yet."

"Okay, okay," I said. "I just hope I don't kill anyone in the process."

Christopher laughed. "I don't think paper planes can kill people," he said. "Maybe give a nasty paper cut, but death is not even on the list of possibilities."

I managed a laugh in return and tried the next plane. It lasted eight seconds. The next, ten. The next, two. That one nearly took someone's eye out.

"All right. I'm done. This was a stupid thing to put on the list anyway." I started to zip up the backpack, feeling flustered and frustrated and like I'd made an idiot of myself in front of a guy I was really starting to like. I flung the bag onto my shoulder and glanced at my phone. We'd wasted an hour, so that was something. At least I hadn't given one thought to karaoke in all that time.

But, oh crap, now I was thinking about it again. What was I going to sing? What if my voice cracked? What if my heel turned in those stupid new boots and I went careening off the stage into someone's shrimp scampi?

"No, no, no. You can't give up!" Christopher said, reaching out unsteadily and grabbing my arm. "Come on, Tess. The whole point of this list is to make you feel better. To make you feel like anything's possible, right? How are you going to feel if you give up on the very first thing?"

I looked into his eyes, and he looked so sincere my heart thumped. The expression on his face was almost desperate. It was as if he was more invested in this whole experiment than I was. Maybe he was. Before I had come along, Christopher had been bored out of his mind, looking at a long week off with nothing to do but watch bad videos on his computer and wishing he'd never agreed to go snowboarding with perfect strangers who were apparently jackasses. I wasn't doing this just for me anymore. I was doing it for him, too. And I kind of liked that he cared so much. Most people probably would have thought that this whole exercise was lame, but Christopher was all in.

"Okay, fine," I said, putting the bag down again and extracting a plane at random. It was a fighter jet–style plane, with a skinny end and two wide wings. I'd even drawn stars on the wings of this one, to pass the time while Christopher was folding another. "One more."

"That's definitely the one." He nodded and readied the timer. I took a deep breath, pulled my arm back, and let the plane fly. This one felt completely different from the first one, and the second it left my hand, my heart seemed to soar right along with it. The plane sailed up and out, and then, almost as if caught on a breeze, it circled around until it was flying parallel to where we were standing. One of the kids down below noticed and pointed up.

"Oooh! Look!"

The other kids in the pool stopped what they were doing to watch, and I was sure that the second they noticed, the plane would dip and crash and disappoint them all, but it didn't. It just kept flying, circling slowly down, until it finally came in for a landing right alongside the shallow end of the pool. Christopher clicked the timer. He stared at the screen.

"What? How long?" I asked as the kids below cheered. I even heard a parent call out, "That was amazing!"

Christopher turned the phone around. It read 31.6 seconds.

My heart leapt. "We did it!"

I jumped up and down and threw my arms around Christopher's

neck. Never in a million years would I have thought I'd get so excited about a paper airplane, but I was. Over thirty seconds! Who even knew it was possible?

"*You* did it!" Christopher said. "You get to cross the first thing off your list!"

I pulled back, and one of his crutches crashed to the floor. He lost his balance and leaned into me, and suddenly I found myself holding him up, his cheek brushing mine. His body was heavy and strong and warm.

"Whoa. Are you okay?" I asked, one hand against his very solid chest.

"Fine. I'm fine." His voice was a bit deeper than usual as he pulled back and looked at me. His gaze flicked from my eyes to my lips and back again, leaving my lips tingling. "Congratulations," he whispered.

"Um, thanks," I whispered.

Suddenly everything around me went fuzzy. The pool noises grew sharper. But above it all my heart pounded like nothing I'd ever heard before.

Christopher pulled me the tiniest bit closer. There was a hitch in my chest. And then, he leaned toward me. And I leaned toward him. We were going to kiss. This was really happening. And I—

The elevator dinged. "Tess!"

Loretta emerged into the hallway and looked around at the fallen crutch, the open backpack, and Christopher, who was trying very hard to spring away from me on one good leg. Taking it all in, Loretta's lips pressed themselves into a thin line.

"I heard someone was throwing paper airplanes into the pool, but I never thought it would be you. I assumed I'd find Lauren up here."

"Sorry," I said. "We just—"

"I suppose I have you to thank for this," Loretta snapped at Christopher, looking him up and down with thinly veiled disdain. "Just because you feel the need to push the envelope, young man, that doesn't mean you need to rope my granddaughter into it."

"Sorry, Loretta." Christopher looked at the floor.

"No! Don't apologize," I protested, confused at her comment. "Loretta, it wasn't—"

"Clean all this up and get back to your room to change," Loretta directed, interrupting. "We're going to dinner in half an hour."

Then she turned and strode off down the hallway toward the stairs.

"Okay. I'm starting to see what you mean about your grandmother being terrifying," Christopher said.

"Thank you!" I replied, throwing up my hands.

And not just terrifying, I thought as I bent to pick up his crutch. *But also a kiss-blocker.*

TESS'S NEW YEAR'S BUCKET LIST

1. Make a paper airplane that actually flies (20 seconds at least) ✓
2. Sing in public
3. Strike up a conversation with a stranger
4. Wear high heels outside the house
5. Make out with a guy whose last name I don't know
6. TP someone's house
7. Get Adam Michel's autograph
8. Get a short, stylish haircut
9. Ski a black diamond slope
10. Eat sushi

CHAPTER NINE

The Sinatra and Pasta dinner was held in one of the smaller party rooms, with round tables draped in red-and-white-checkered tablecloths. Wine bottles had been repurposed as candleholders at the center of each table, and the candles dripped wax onto the cut-glass plates beneath them. Waiters dressed in black tuxedos served heaping plates of spaghetti and meatballs, chicken parmesan, and Caesar salads. I sat between Lauren and Loretta and tried to enjoy the food—which all smelled delicious—but it was impossible. My stomach was—big shock here—filled to the brim with butterflies.

At least I'd crossed one thing off my list. Even after getting caught by Loretta and *not* getting kissed, it had felt beyond satisfying to take that Sharpie and make a big old check mark next to #1. I was officially on my way.

"Holy wow, Tess, if you're going to keep doing that, at least do it with some rhythm," Lauren said, slapping a hand down over mine on the table.

My heart skipped a startled beat, and I looked down. I was

holding a fork in my flattened hand and didn't realize until that moment that I'd been tapping it against the table.

"Sorry," I said, and withdrew my hands into my lap. Instantly, my feet began to bounce. But at least that wasn't as noticeable.

"Sheesh. You're a mess." Lauren took a huge bite out of a garlic knot and eyed me curiously. "Why did you even agree to this karaoke thing? Did that Christopher kid dare you or something?"

"Shhh!" I admonished, glancing over at Loretta, who was still chatting up the woman sitting on her other side, thank goodness. I didn't need our grandmother blaming more things on Christopher and getting it into her head that the two of us shouldn't be hanging out together. "I don't take dares anymore. That was the old me."

"That you was a lot more fun," Lauren shot back, but not nastily. More matter-of-factly. And I didn't entirely disagree.

When I was little, I'd been known for never turning down a dare. One time, on the playground behind school, I'd even eaten a dead bug when Sebastian Domaskis had told everyone I was too scared. (And then had spent the rest of the day puking up my guts. But at least Sebastian had puked, too. And before I did. He deserved it, the little jerk.) What had happened to that version of me, though? Not that I wanted to go around eating dead bugs or anything. But I'd definitely become a lot more timid somewhere between then and now.

I looked at Loretta again. My grandmother seemed to have made a new best friend in the middle-aged lady who had come along with her husband and another couple. The two of them had found common ground when the woman had brought up her latest trip to Europe, and they had been comparing notes on the best hotels in the Pyrenees ever since. It was really amazing, how easy it was for Loretta to talk to strangers—to make friends out of everyone she met. Everyone who worked for her loved, or at least respected, her, and from what I could tell, she loved or respected them right back.

"I just thought it would be good to try some new things," I said with a shrug, and took a sip from my water glass. I wasn't ready to tell my sister about the list. There was no doubt in my mind that Lauren would find the whole idea mockable. Lauren was the kind of person who just did things. She didn't make lists. She didn't even double-think her decisions. If I was an over-thinker, Lauren was an under-thinker. A non-thinker. She was a doer.

And I'd never seen her make a list in my life.

"I think that's cool," Lauren said. "I'm impressed."

A warm and fuzzy feeling erupted inside my chest. It was nice to feel like my sister was proud of me for once. Over on the small stage in the corner, the singer—who actually looked a lot like Frank Sinatra if I squinted—launched into "New York, New York." He looked so confident up there, holding his microphone casually, tipping his head back and closing his eyes, snapping his fingers to keep the beat.

"How do people *do* that?" I whispered to my sister.

"Some people are just natural-born performers."

"Maybe I'm one and I don't even know it?" I said hopefully.

Lauren scoffed. "Doubtful."

I groaned and slumped.

"Sorry. I'm just messing with you. I'm sure it will be fine. You just get up there, pick a short song, and it'll be over before you know it. That's the thing about karaoke. You might be bad, but within three songs, there will definitely be someone worse. Plus no one is focused on you because they're all so focused on what they're gonna sing." She patted me twice on the shoulder. "Just be forgettable, that's my advice. Don't try too hard, and no one will remember it tomorrow."

Don't try too hard. Did she even know me? The very idea of not trying gave me hives.

"So, girls. Do you know who absolutely *loves* Frank Sinatra?" Loretta asked out of nowhere, finally turning her attention to the granddaughters she'd forced to come here so they could enjoy "family time."

"Our dad?" Lauren said moodily.

"Exactly!"

"We know," I said, twirling some spaghetti onto my fork unenthusiastically. "He plays his music all the time in the car. I've never understood it. Wasn't Frank Sinatra, like, very before his time?"

"Yes, in fact, he was, but your father got into his music because he was your grandfather's favorite," Loretta said, and took a sip of her wine. "Most kids would have shunned their dad's musical interests, but not your father. He was always such a good son—so kind and so loyal. Instead of making your grandfather feel like an old fool for his choice in music, he listened and ended up appreciating it as much as your grandfather did."

"Yeah, well. He lost that whole loyalty thing somewhere along the way," Lauren muttered, ripping into another garlic knot.

"Lauren! That's not fair. Nor is it appropriate," Loretta said, and my heart squeezed.

"Call it what you want, Loretta, but it doesn't change the fact that *he's* the one who's leaving," Lauren said, and swallowed hard.

"So forgive me if I don't want to sit here and get all poetic about how amazing and loyal he is."

And just like that, Lauren shoved her chair back from the table, got up, and stormed away.

"Lauren! Get back here!" Loretta said through her teeth, clearly trying not to make a scene in front of her guests.

But Lauren either didn't hear her or was ignoring her, and she swept right out of the room, just as the crooner in the corner was belting out the most famous line of his song:

"If I can MAKE it there, I'll make it ANYWHERE!"

I sat back in my seat, hard. I couldn't believe it. All this time, in the many months since our parents had sat us down and told us they were getting a divorce, Lauren had never gotten emotional about it. Not once. Her completely blasé attitude had been pissing me off forever. So why now? Why here?

Loretta reached for her wine again, and I saw that my grandmother's hand was shaking.

"I'm sorry, Loretta. I guess she's just upset about this whole thing."

"It's all right, dear. It's not your fault," Loretta said, giving me a wan smile. "It's going to take everyone a while to adjust to this new normal."

But that was the thing—I had been sure that my sister already *had* adjusted. That she'd never really cared to begin with. Had I been wrong this entire time? Had I missed something? Or was my sister just the greatest actor of all time?

"Well, it's too bad," Loretta said, perking up again. "Now she's going to miss Campfire Bingo."

Alarm bells went off in my head. Lauren was supposed to

run interference with Loretta for the rest of the night so I could go change into my boots and sing karaoke. Now, my wingman was gone.

"Campfire Bingo?" I asked, trying to sound casual. "What's Campfire Bingo?"

"You'll see," Loretta said. "Don't worry. The kids always seem to enjoy it. And there's hot chocolate!"

"Where is it? What time does it start?" I asked, dreading the answer.

"Outside around the fire pit," Loretta told me, cutting a small piece of chicken. "Promptly at nine o'clock."

$$\bullet\ \bullet\ \bullet$$

So there I was. Playing bingo under the stars. With about two dozen second graders and their parents. When Loretta said, "the kids always seem to enjoy it," she meant the *kids*. As in overtired little humans with snot running down their faces and a serious inability to sit still. Yes, the stars overhead were lovely, and the fire roared impressively. Plus there was not just hot chocolate but s'mores of all kinds. But still. Not another person my age was in sight. Unless you counted the college-aged nanny who had a toddler pulling on her braids across the fire while she tried to keep track of three other kids' bingo cards. Which I did not.

"N twenty-two! That's N twenty-two!" shouted the gentleman in charge of the snowballs. That was what they were calling the little white balls that came out of the bingo tumbler, which had been decorated to look like a snowy mountain. There was really no detail overlooked around here. My grandmother ran a tight holiday ship.

I looked down at my card, which was shaped like a snowflake. No N 22.

"Bingo!" a little kid named Ethan shouted, jumping up and down with his arms in the air and then striking some semi-disturbing weight lifter poses like he was a pro-wrestler or something.

"See? Isn't this fun?" Loretta said, leaning toward me as she cleared her own bingo board.

"Ethan's sure having a good time," I replied.

I only knew Ethan's name because his mother had been shouting it at him for the last twenty minutes straight. *Ethan, stop hitting your sister! Ethan, get your finger out of your nose!! Ethan, don't eat that! Ethan! Ethan! Ethan!*

Now he ran over to the bingo table, trampling everyone and everything in his way, to pick up his prize—a brand-new, light-up Bluetooth speaker.

"I already have one of these!" he wailed, and threw it at the ground. Everyone around the fire heard the loud *crack* of the speaker inside the box breaking.

God, kids really sucked sometimes.

"Ethan! Say you're sorry!"

There was a bit of a distraction while Ethan threw a tantrum and his mother tried to corral him, so I took the opportunity to check my phone. There were a bunch of texts from Christopher.

> I got us a table. Have you begged out of bingo yet?
> It's starting. Where are you?
> The song list is filling up fast. Should I sign you up?
> What do you want to sing? Did you decide???
> OK I signed you up. Are you coming?

This was a nightmare. I both really needed to go and really didn't want to go from the depth of my soul. Maybe I should just say forget it. Maybe this list thing wasn't meant to be and I should just sit here under the heat lamps and this glorious fleece blanket and play bingo with the brats. But then I thought of the list. And of Christopher's face when he told me the plane had flown for over thirty seconds.

And of Christopher's lips when he'd almost kissed me.

Okay. I really needed to go.

But how? There was no sneaking away from Loretta when she was sitting three inches from me.

I glanced over at her, and she quickly looked away, studying her blank bingo board as if it held the meaning of life. Had she been trying to sneak a peek at my phone? What had she seen? Loretta was a lot of things, but I had never pegged her for a snoop.

"Is that your sister? Is everything all right?" she asked.

So she hadn't seen anything. And her question made me pause. A tiny tingle of adrenaline raced up my spine. Lauren may have ditched me, but was it possible she could still get me out of Campfire Bingo?

"Actually, yeah, that was her," I lied through my teeth. "She wants to talk. Is it okay if I go?"

I shoved my phone away in case she decided she wanted to see the messages. Loretta started to speak, but then the shouting on the other side of the fire got louder. A lot louder.

"I don't *want* another board! I want my prize!" Ethan was shouting.

"You got a prize. Just say thank you and let's go," his mother begged.

"I want a *good* prize!"

Ethan dove into the huge box, wrapped up like a present, that held the prizes, and started flinging smaller boxes out onto the ground. All of which held the exact same Bluetooth speaker he'd just won.

Loretta looked torn for half a second, then said, "I should deal with this. Yes, go. I'll see you girls in the morning."

Then she shoved herself out of her Adirondack chair with surprising dexterity and marched around the fire to deal—diplomatically, I was sure—with young Ethan.

And I was free!

To sing in front of a room full of people.

Gulp.

CHAPTER TEN

"Next up, please welcome to the stage, Tess Sachs, singing . . . 'Wonderful Christmastime'!"

My body completely shut down. I'd been waiting for this moment ever since I'd walked into the room almost an hour ago—hell, I'd been waiting for it all day. But somehow, hearing the cheesy DJ dude in the comically oversized sunglasses call my name was still a total shock to my system. Also, "Wonderful Christmastime"? What was Christopher thinking?

I looked over my shoulder at him—we were seated at the tiniest round two-top table I'd ever seen—and he shrugged. "I figured it was seasonal and easy to carry," he said. "You're the one who wouldn't answer your texts."

"It's fine," I said. At least I knew the song. It was one of my mom's favorite Christmas classics. Plus, it was really more talking than singing. It was kind of a genius choice, actually. "Thanks for getting me on the list." I hoped I sounded sincere. At the moment I really had zero clue *what* I was feeling. Faint, mostly.

"Tess Sachs, are you still out there?" The DJ put his iPad over his eyes, as if he was using it to shade the sun, and slowly scanned the crowd. "Going once . . ."

Christopher leaned across the small tabletop, where each of us had been nursing root beers while we waited for my ultimate demise. "You can do this, Tess. Come on."

"Going twice . . ."

"In five minutes it'll all be over."

He sounded like my sister. Was that what everyone here was thinking? *Just get it over with*? I wondered if anyone in this room thought this sort of public humiliation was actually fun.

"Yeah, and I might be dead."

"Unlikely," Christopher shot back.

"Going . . . going . . ."

"Think of the list, Type A!" Christopher urged.

"I'm here!"

I stood up, and my knees almost collapsed underneath me. Also, my voice cracked spectacularly on the word *here*, which did not bode well. But then the crowd turned to look at me and people started to cheer and, well, there was no going back. I made my way toward the stage, tripping once and catching myself on the back of some poor girl's chair, before finally making it to the stairs. I'd thought I was doing pretty well in my new heels, but I had to seriously concentrate just to get up the three steps in one piece. Then, the DJ was handing me the microphone, the music was starting, and there were the words, lighting up on the TV in front of me.

I looked out at the audience, trying to spot Christopher, but the brightest light ever constructed by man shone directly in my face, basically blinding me to everyone and everything beyond the first row of tables. I was on my own.

And so, I started to sing.

My voice was . . . not good. It was quiet. And breathy. And not in the least bit confident. I was tanking. I could feel it. The group of girlfriends at the first table was actually squirming in discomfort. This was a disaster. But I was doing it. And like Christopher had said, in five minutes it would be over.

I looked at the TV, as if I didn't have this song memorized backwards and forwards, and there I saw it. The chorus. Okay. If I was ever going to save this, the time was now. I closed my eyes and just belted out the chorus. I pretended I was in my shower back home and just sang. As loudly as I could without passing out. And then, the most miraculous thing happened.

Somebody cheered.

Yeah. I'm not kidding. Somebody, not Christopher, actually cheered. And then people began clapping to the beat. And that's when something dawned on me. It wasn't just me singing up there alone. We were all in this together. I was just the person who happened to be on the stage at that moment. But a bunch of those people out there had sung before me. And some of them would sing after me. Karaoke wasn't a single-person event. This was a group thing. A team thing. And I wasn't about to let my team down.

I kept singing. And I opened my eyes. I'm pretty sure I even smiled.

"Come on, everyone, join in!" I shouted before the chorus began again. "You know the words."

And the crowd started to sing with me. And I *really* wasn't the center of attention anymore. I waved the audience on, encouraging them, and noticed that the guy from the coffee shop—Damon— was sitting at one of the front tables near the door, and he was one of the people clapping and singing enthusiastically along. When our eyes met, he gave me a quick thumbs-up, and a little thrill went through me.

A cute boy was enjoying my song. The song that was almost over. Just one more time through the chorus and this whole nightmare—was it a nightmare?—would be over.

When I finally hit the last note, I was so relieved and giddy, I started laughing and threw one hand in the air. Everyone cheered. Well, I don't know if it was everyone—I still couldn't see eighty percent of the room—but it felt like everyone. My first time singing karaoke was a success.

But even more importantly? I'd just crossed two more items off my list. I couldn't wait to find Christopher again and celebrate.

• • •

Walking back through the crowd, I felt one hundred percent the opposite of how I'd felt going up to the stage. I weighed zero pounds. My chest was all puffed up and full of helium. There was nothing I couldn't do. People slapped me on my back and yelled encouraging things like "nice job!" and "get it, girl!" and "that didn't suck!" I was smiling so hard my cheeks hurt.

"That was amazing!" Christopher shouted.

He pushed himself up from his chair, bracing both hands on the table, and reached in to hug me. I managed to somehow balance his weight without tottering on my high heels and wrapped my arms fully around him. It was, possibly, the most perfect moment of my life. If doing stuff I'd never done before always felt like this, I was going to be doing new things much more often.

"You did it!" he said, pulling back, but keeping one hand on my lower back. His cast leg was crooked beneath him, making him look like a cute flamingo. I could feel the warmth of his palm through my T-shirt. "How does it feel?"

"Oh my God, so good!" I cried, pressing my fingertips to my cheeks. "I can't stop smiling."

"Congratulations. That was so great. Everyone was really into it. And getting them to sing along with you was genius."

"Thank you. I'm just glad I didn't fall off the stage." I gestured at my shoes and laughed.

"Unreal," Christopher said, and lowered himself back into his chair. "You just checked off two more things from your list. Three in one day. We're on a roll."

I liked this *we* thing. It was really kind of amazing how all-in Christopher was on this whole experiment.

"Yeah, we totally are."

I sat down next to him again and reached for my root beer just as the DJ announced that they were going to be taking a break and he'd be back in ten minutes. The volume of the conversation around us swelled as people pored over the list of songs and decided what to sing next. I sensed someone standing next to my chair and noticed Christopher's face go stiff. I looked up. It was Damon. His dark hair was pushed back from his face, and he wore a plaid cowboy-style shirt with the little snaps down the front that most people couldn't have pulled off, but it looked good on him.

"Hey . . . Tess, right?" he said. "I just wanted to tell you, you did great." He pointed a thumb over his shoulder at the stage, then shoved both hands into the front pockets of his jeans. "I'm Damon. From the coffee shop? Remember? I'm Tarek's cousin. I think he's been hanging out with your sister, Lauren, right?"

"Yes! Hi! I didn't know you and Tarek were related." I think I was still a little high on adrenaline, because I couldn't exactly think straight. But Damon did look a little bit like Tarek—only Damon hadn't gotten those bright blue eyes his cousin had been blessed with. His were light brown. And he was thinner and wirier than Tarek, who had more of a football player's build. "It's nice to see you again."

Damon nodded, and his gaze flicked past me toward Christopher. "Hey."

"Oh, I'm sorry, this is Christopher."

"S'up man?" Damon said, glancing down at Christopher's cast. "Bad luck."

"Something like that," Christopher said.

The air was so cold between them, I could have been back outside under the stars at Campfire Bingo. But without the fire.

"Anyway." Damon returned his attention to me. "If you stop by the café in the morning, I'll get you a coffee on me. That performance deserves a reward."

"Um, thanks," I said, wanting to kill the awkward. "Maybe I will. And thanks for coming over. I appreciate it. I was really nervous."

"Really? I couldn't tell," he said. "Like, not at all."

I blushed and looked down. I couldn't help it. I wasn't used to all this attention.

"Anyway, I'll let you get back to . . . ya know. See you soon," Damon said.

"You too," I replied. He lifted a hand and walked away, heading back to rejoin his friends.

I could feel Christopher staring at me, so I grabbed my root beer and took a long sip. I wasn't sure why, but I couldn't seem to make myself look him in the eye.

"I just talked to a stranger," I said, hazarding a quick glance. "Does that count as number four?"

"Not a chance," he replied. "That guy came over here to talk to you. Totally does not count."

"Oh," I said, a little thrown by his businesslike tone. "Good point."

Christopher checked his phone and got up. "My parents are looking for me," he said, tossing some money on the table and shoving his phone into his back pocket. "I gotta go."

"Wait. Really? Just like that?" I said.

"Yeah. Sorry. I'll see you," he said. He gathered up his crutches and started to move away from the table, but paused after a few steps and turned back. "You really did do great up there, Tess."

"Thanks," I said, totally unsure of how to feel. Had something gone wrong here? Had I done something? Was I stupid to think that I might get a second chance at that kiss?

"I'll see you tomorrow," he said.

And then he was gone.

TESS'S NEW YEAR'S BUCKET LIST

1. Make a paper airplane that actually flies (20 seconds at least) ✔
2. Sing in public ✔
3. Strike up a conversation with a stranger
4. Wear high heels outside the house ✔
5. Make out with a guy whose last name I don't know
6. TP someone's house
7. Get Adam Michel's autograph
8. Get a short, stylish haircut
9. Ski a black diamond slope
10. Eat sushi

CHAPTER ELEVEN

DECEMBER 29

The next morning I woke up feeling like I could basically conquer the world. It was amazing how performing in front of a crowd had completely shifted my attitude about everything. I smiled at myself in the mirror while brushing my teeth. I blew my hair until it was totally dry and left it down instead of tying it into my usual ponytail. And when my sister grumbled at me about my perkiness, I just ignored her and walked out of the room—although I may have slammed the door *just* a little bit harder than necessary.

Downstairs at breakfast, instead of getting my usual—pancakes and bacon—I decided to join the line at the omelet station. I had always liked cheese in my scrambled eggs. Why not get them in omelet form? And maybe I'd have them throw some tomatoes in there, too. Go crazy!

The only thing putting any sort of negative tinge on my good mood was the way Christopher had up and left so abruptly the night before. But maybe it was nothing. He'd broken his leg just a few days ago, and I'd dragged him around town all morning and out of bed in the afternoon. Maybe he was just exhausted. That was probably all it was.

I was waiting for a couple of minutes on line for food when the girl from the international buffet on my first night here stepped up behind me—the one who hadn't seemed to be sitting with anyone she knew. She was wearing an outfit I could never pull off—brightly striped tights, a plaid shirt, and a fuzzy white sweater. I would have looked like a clown in that combo, but she looked stylish and cool. She had black-brown curly hair cut short around her ears, and light brown skin that glowed as if she was lit from the inside. Once again, she was engrossed in a book, but I couldn't tell what it was because of the angle at which she held it—flat in front of her, her head bowed so she could read.

Was she still into *The Seven Siren Stars,* or was she on to the sequel, *The Eighth Earth*? And if it was *The Eighth Earth,* had she gotten to the part where Simon had to cut off Aramaya's left hand to save them all from the three-headed gorgon and an eternity of endless night? She bit her lip and turned the page. The line inched forward. My heart was starting to pound. I could just ask her. I *should* just ask her. She was clearly a book nerd, like me. What was the worst that could happen?

"Whatcha reading?" I blurted out.

The girl looked up. Was it just me, or had I sounded like a kindergartener just then? Ugh, she probably thought I was a freak.

For half a second she eyed me a bit warily, and I thought she was going to bolt or tell me off or just ignore me. But then, she lifted the book so I could see the cover. It *was The Eighth Earth,* but it had a weird cover I'd never seen before. "I've just started it," she said. "But it's *so* good."

She had an English accent. There was literally nothing I loved more on this planet than an English accent. I endured bad rom-coms with my mom sometimes just so I could hear Hugh Grant talk.

"Oh my God, I'm so jealous," I told her. "I would kill to get to read that again for the first time."

"Really?" she said, brightening slightly. Her shoulders also relaxed, as if she'd just decided that I was maybe not a psychopath. "I loved the last one and I feel like this one *has* to be a disappointment after that."

I shook my head. "Nope. No way. This one is soooo much better."

"All right, all right! Don't get my hopes up *too* high!" she said with a laugh. Her curls shuddered when she laughed, making me wish my hair wasn't so dang straight and boring. But then, I was going to chop it off, right? Maybe within a couple of days I'd also have enviable hair. A girl could dream. And be simultaneously terrified of said dream.

"You're right. Sorry," I said. "I'll shut up now."

"Next!"

It was my turn at the front of the line. I ordered an omelet with cheddar and roasted tomatoes. The girl put a bookmark in to hold her page and hugged the book to her chest.

"It's just, I've never been a big reader," she told me, blushing. "Until recently, I'd only really read fashion mags and blogs or music columns. But someone recommended this series to me, and I had *no* idea. It's so engrossing! I can't ever put it down."

"Welcome to the life of a habitual reader," I told her.

"I'm Carina," she said. "I've been dragged here against my will for my dad's latest work trip."

"Tess," I replied. "Sent here against my will to spend time with my grandmother."

No need to bring up the divorce. I didn't have to tell my sad history to every single person I met on this trip. Thinking this made me think of Christopher, and I glanced up and down the buffet again. No sign of him. No sign of his parents.

"My sympathies," she said jokingly.

"Mine, too. For you, I mean."

The chef behind the counter took her order—egg-white omelet with spinach and feta—and then we stood aside to wait for our food.

"So, are you going skiing today?" Carina asked. "My dad's been so busy, we haven't gone out on the slopes yet, and I hate to go alone."

"I wasn't planning on it," I told her. "My grandmother wants us to go to some high tea or something with her."

"Us?" she asked.

"Oh, me and my sister," I said just as Lauren herself walked through the double doors with Tarek and . . . Damon? What were they all doing together? And how had Lauren gotten up and showered and made herself look that good that fast? It would always be a mystery to me. The three of them glanced around, and when Lauren saw me, she pointed me out. To Damon. He grinned and started weaving around other diners toward me and Carina.

"Oh, God," I said.

"What?" Carina looked around, baffled.

"Guy. There. Coming. Here."

"Okay, you just went totally Cro-Magnon on me," she said, her brows knitting.

"Hey, Tess!" Damon greeted me, all dimples and confidence. I noticed he wasn't wearing his Best Bean polo short or his name tag. He was, instead, wearing a very nice and form-fitting blue ski sweater and had his long hair down around his shoulders, which kind of made him look like a model in an outdoorsy catalog. The whole effect was making me sweat just the tiniest bit. Clearly he was off duty right now.

"Hilo," I said. "I mean, hello. Hi. What's up? I thought you were working."

"They doubled up shifts by mistake, so I got the morning off." Damon looked at Carina. "Hey. I'm Damon. Are you a friend of Tess's?"

"We just met, but I like to think we've formed a deep and impenetrable bond," Carina said. Damon just looked confused. "Yes. We're friends," she added slowly. "I'm Carina."

"Nice to meet you." He turned his attention back to me, hands in the pockets of his black sweatpants. "So me and Tarek and Lauren were gonna go hit the slopes. You wanna come?"

I actually flinched, I was so taken aback. "Um . . . we can't go skiing," I told him, just as the chef handed over my plate. I took it from him, the steam still rising from the eggs. "My grandmother has plans for us all day. Me and my sister, I mean. Not, you know. . . . you. Or Tarek. Or anyone. Else." Why couldn't I form a normal sentence?

"Screw the plans."

I jumped. Lauren had somehow snuck up behind me and was now eating a piece of sausage wrapped in a pancake like it was a taco.

"I want to go skiing," she added, her mouth full. Tarek sidled up behind her, gnawing on a bagel. Damon and Tarek standing next to each other was almost too much hotness to handle this early in the morning.

"I . . ."

I glanced at Carina, who had also just gotten her food. She looked at me hopefully. She wanted to go skiing, too, and it seemed like she was hoping to get roped into this new group plan. I thought of Christopher, wishing he could join us, too, but clearly that wasn't in the cards. Where was he, though? Still in bed? It wasn't like him to miss breakfast.

I knew what he'd tell me if he was here, though—this was my opportunity to cross another item off my list—ski a black diamond run. And I could do it with my sister, so if I died, there'd be someone there to deal with my remains.

"Sure, I guess," I said, and Tarek whooped. "Can Carina come, too?"

"You're Carina?" Lauren said, looking her up and down.

"And you're the sister?" Carina replied, looking Lauren up and down right back.

"Oooh! You have an accent!" Lauren said, excited. "What part of Britain are you from?"

"The cool part," Carina shot back.

Lauren barked a laugh. "I like her," my sister proclaimed. "Fine by me."

"Sweet!" Damon said. "Let me grab some grub. I'm starving."

He turned and walked over to the carb station. Tarek gave my sister a quick kiss on the cheek and squeezed her arms. "I just have to check my schedule for next week before we go." Then he bounded off, too.

"Go where?"

I jumped again. This time it was Loretta. Was everyone in my family this good at sneaking up on people?

"Loretta!" Lauren exclaimed with a big smile. "Tess and I

were just making plans with Tarek and his cousin to go skiing for the day."

Loretta's lips formed that thin, stern line I was getting so used to seeing on this trip. "Girls, I don't think that's such a good idea."

"Why not?" Lauren asked. "This is a ski resort, isn't it? And we haven't been skiing once since we've been here."

We both looked at Loretta hopefully. Lauren did have a point. Not that I had ever planned to hit the slopes on this trip before making my list with Christopher, but it did feel kind of lame being here and never venturing up the mountain.

"We still haven't found something for Tess to wear on New Year's Eve. And we have reservations for high tea this afternoon, remember," Loretta replied.

I exchanged a look with Lauren. Loretta now had on her no-nonsense look—raised chin, lowered eyelashes. There was no combatting that.

"Your granddaughters were nice enough to offer to accompany me, Ms. Sachs," Carina said, jumping in. "As you know, my father has been otherwise occupied since we got here, and I'm still pretty much a novice. I think having them out there with me will be a tremendous help."

I stared at Carina. Lauren stared at Carina. What the hell was this? And how did she know my grandmother well enough to start trying to talk her into things?

"Oh. I see. Of course, Miss Granger." Was Loretta . . . flustered? "Girls, please do make sure this guest has everything she needs."

"Um . . . okay," I said. "We will, Loretta."

"Have fun, all of you." Then she took my hand and held it tightly, looking into my eyes. "And Tess, remember what happened to your friend Christopher. Stick with your sister and be careful."

"Okay," I said warily. The intensity she was giving off was weird. And, well, *intense.* Like she was trying to tell me something else. Something she didn't want to say in front of Carina, maybe?

She held my gaze for an extra second, until it got *really* uncomfortable. Then she finally gave us a quick nod and turned to go. She greeted other guests on her way out, as she always did, but something about her posture seemed off. It was almost like she was disappointed—more than that—crestfallen. Was it that big a deal that she was going to miss high tea?

Or was it that big of a deal that she wasn't going to spend the afternoon with us? Was Loretta . . . lonely?

Or maybe she was just really worried I was going to get hurt out there. A thought that did not make me any more confident about this whole black diamond idea.

"Okay, how did you do that and can you teach us your magic?" Lauren asked Carina.

Carina smirked, but looked at me. "Let's go eat before this gets cold. We're going to need sustenance if we're going skiing. Plus we *need* to talk about book one."

"Over here!" Damon called out from the end of a table nearby, waving me and Carina down.

And together we walked off, leaving my sister behind all by her lonesome.

Not on my list, but for sure another first in my life.

• • •

I was not dressed for skiing, so I went back up to our room to change, and quickly checked off one more item from the list: *Strike up a conversation with a stranger.* (Thanks to my big leap on the omelet line with Carina.) Look at that. I hadn't meant to go in any kind of order, but I'd checked off the first four tasks on the list anyway. The next one was: *Make out with a guy whose last name I don't know.* I blushed and shoved the list away. Not quite ready to think about that one just yet. In fact, if I was going in order, that definitely should have been last.

The thing was, I wasn't much of a kissing person. Or a dating person. Or a person who attracted members of the opposite sex. I'd been kissed before. At a party at my friend Isabel's last year, we'd played a fairly lame game of spin the bottle where I'd landed on Alex Fletcher, which made basically everyone jealous because he's the hottest guy in my class. We'd kissed for exactly sixty seconds, and it had been completely underwhelming. All slobbery and awkward. Then, this past fall, I'd gone out with Frankie Pintaro for a whole month, and we'd done some stuff. Nothing super interesting, though. He was sweet and cute, but I didn't have huge feelings for him or anything, which made the whole thing kind of meh.

So, I wasn't exactly experienced, and I wasn't one of those girls who could just see a cute guy at a party, make out with him, and move on. I had nothing against the girls who could do that. I just wasn't built that way. I was either too shy or too tense or too type A, I guess, for random smooching. I wanted a connection with someone before I kissed him.

Like the connection I had with Christopher. Had he really been about to kiss me yesterday? The more time passed, the more certain I was that I'd imagined the whole thing. But I *really* wanted to kiss him. Unfortunately, he wouldn't count for the list, since I already knew his last name.

It seemed I was going to have to get over this whole connection thing. At least I would if I was going to complete my list.

The door to the room opened just as I was pulling on my ski pants, and I gave a yelp.

"It's just me!" Lauren said, but closed the door quickly. "Sorry. I figured I'd check if you needed help."

"Getting dressed? I've kind of been doing that on my own for a while now." I zipped up the hidden zipper and tucked my base layer turtleneck in.

"No, I mean . . . Damon's totally into you. You know that, right?"

My body heat skyrocketed so fast, I was super glad for the sweat-wicking fabric I'd just put on. "What? No, he's not. What are you talking about?"

I went into the bathroom to slather sunblock on my face, which already looked sunburned thanks to all the embarrassment. Lauren followed. She leaned against the doorjamb, her arms crossed over her chest.

"Yeah, he totally is." She smiled at my clearly flustered self as I shoved a headband into my hair and it fell right off the back of my head. "Sheesh. Calm down. He's just a guy."

"Just a hot guy," I blurted out. "Possibly the hottest I've ever met."

"After Tarek," she said, sidling into the room. "Or maybe third, after a certain blond dude in a leg cast?"

She reached for a lip gloss wand and raised one eyebrow at me in the mirror.

Christopher. My heart fluttered at the very thought of him. Maybe I should tell Lauren about the almost-kiss? I bet she'd have some advice. But what if I'd imagined the whole thing? What if Christopher didn't even know I existed as anything other than a person to distract him from his boredom? He'd bailed right after

I'd sung my karaoke song last night and hadn't texted me all morning. Was that the way you treated someone you wanted to kiss? I tugged my phone out of my side zip pocket now just to check, and nope. Nada.

"I don't . . . I mean . . . I just met Christopher. And I've said two words to Damon."

"Well, all he could talk about was how *amazing* you were at karaoke last night," Lauren said, leaning in to apply her lip gloss. "I'm sorry I bailed, by the way." She met my eyes for half a second. "Loretta just kind of pissed me off."

"Yeah. I picked up on that." I couldn't believe Lauren was apologizing to me for anything without being forced, but I decided not to harp on that for now.

She put the lip gloss down and turned around, leaning her butt against the countertop and bracing her hands on either side of her hips. She stared down at her boots and, for the first time in forever, actually looked vulnerable. "This divorce stuff sucks sometimes, you know? And it just hits me out of nowhere. Like, I'll be fine and then *boof*, it hits me that nothing's ever going to be the same again."

I froze. This was the first time Lauren had ever talked to me about how she really felt about our parents' split. I was worried that if I moved an inch, I'd burst the tenuous bubble that had formed around us and she'd clam up. My pulse thrummed in my wrists. I really needed to talk to her about this. I couldn't let the moment pass us by.

"I know exactly what you mean," I said quietly. "It's the same for me."

She was quiet for a second, and then she lifted her chin. "Sometimes I wish they'd just suck it up, you know? They're supposed to be the adults in this family. They're always telling us to be responsible, so why can't they?"

I shrugged. "I don't know. I guess they must just be so unhappy that responsibility doesn't matter anymore?"

"Then screw it. We shouldn't have to be responsible, either."

She grabbed a lipstick out of her makeup bag, uncapped it, and brought it toward my face. I leaned back, away from her. "What are you doing?"

"You need lip color. You look like a corpse."

"Thanks a lot!" I said with a laugh.

"Just trust me on this, okay? For once?"

I looked into her eyes. We were actually occupying a small room together and not fighting or snipping or mocking each other. The least I could do was seal it with her lipstick.

"Fine," I said.

I let her apply the lipstick for me, then looked in the mirror. She was right. I did look much less corpse-like.

"You can talk to me about Mom and Dad, you know," I told her. "Anytime."

She rolled her eyes, and I thought our bonding moment was over, but then she said, "Thanks. Maybe I will."

And we were off.

• • •

Down in the lobby, I couldn't help glancing over at Christopher's usual couch near the fireplace as I tugged on my gloves. Sure enough, there he was, all set up with his stack of books, his laptop, and what appeared to be a steaming cup of coffee. Tarek and Damon were waiting by the door with our skis and ski boots ready to go, but I hesitated, feeling nervous and . . . was that guilt tinting my veins? It just felt wrong, going out for a fun day on the slopes while Christopher had to sit here by himself and do nothing. Part of me wanted to just forget it and go camp out by the fire with him. Would that be so wrong?

Answer: Yes. Yes, it would be so wrong. Because I had committed to completing my list, and I wasn't going to let myself down.

I wished he hadn't broken his leg so he could come with us. But then, if he hadn't broken his leg, there was a decent chance I never would have met him. Life was weird that way.

"Give me a second," I said to Lauren.

She leveled me with a knowing look. "You could always strap him into a baby carrier on your back and bring him with you," she joked.

"I'm laughing on the inside," I said flatly.

She air-kissed me, then traipsed over to join the guys.

"Hey!" I said, coming up behind Christopher, who was leaning back against the arm of the couch.

He craned his neck to smile up at me. "Hi! I was just doing some research for your list. Turns out there are not one, not two, but three sushi restaurants within a ten-mile radius of this Podunk town. Who knew?"

"Really? Cool." I felt even guiltier now. He'd been sitting here, working on *my* self-improvement project, and I was going to leave him alone all day. I sat down in my usual chair, adjacent to the couch, and leaned forward. "So, good news, I crossed something else off my list."

"No way. Which one?" he asked, sitting up a bit.

"I talked to a stranger." His face clouded unexpectedly, and

I wondered if he was remembering the whole Damon thing last night. "Her name's Carina," I added quickly. "And we have the same taste in books."

"That's cool." Christopher grinned. "So, four down, six to go. I'm impressed." Then, for the first time, he seemed to notice my outfit. "Are you going skiing?" he asked.

"Yeah. My sister was all over me about it this morning," I said, pointedly leaving out any mention of Damon and Tarek. "And Carina wanted to go, too. I figured I would try to ski a black diamond."

"Wow. You're really on a roll."

I gave a comical bow of my head. "I do what I can."

"Tess! You coming?" Lauren called out.

I looked up and saw that Carina had joined my sister and the guys, all decked out in a pink-and-white ski jacket and matching helmet and gloves. Christopher turned, too, and the second he saw the group near the door, his expression shifted.

"They're going with you?" he said, facing me again.

I knew exactly who he meant by "they." The two fairly handsome ski dudes wearing professional-looking gear and laughing like they hadn't a care between them.

"Yeah, it was supposed to be the four of us until I invited Carina," I told him, wanting to prove that it wasn't like I had angled to spend the day with Damon.

"Like a double date?" he said with forced casualness, looking back at his laptop.

"No. Nothing like a double date. I mean, yeah, my sister likes Tarek. Like, a lot. So, it's probably a date to her. But not for me. I'm mostly going to hang out with Carina. I don't even know Damon."

I tend to ramble when I'm nervous.

"You're right," Christopher said, his expression serious. "You don't know Damon."

Something about the way he said it set off little alarm bells at the back of my neck. "Do *you* know Damon?" I asked. Last night at karaoke, they hadn't seemed to know one another, but had I read that whole conversation wrong?

Christopher looked like he was on the verge of saying something, but then his face shut down and he looked away. "You know what? Forget it. It's nothing. Have fun."

"No, no, no. There's no 'forget it' now." There was a tight, panicky feeling rising in my throat. "Christopher, what's going on?"

He glanced over at the door, then shifted forward slightly on the couch and leaned toward me. "He's the guy," he said urgently, his voice low.

"*What* guy?" I asked, baffled.

"The guy who ran me off the mountain," he said. "The guy who broke my leg."

My heart completely dropped. "What? No! Damon?"

"Sorry, but it's true."

"I don't understand," I said, my mind whirling. I had pictured the guy who ran Christopher off the mountain. In my head he was a big, jock-y jerkface with a square chin and an evil laugh. He was completely not Damon. "Why didn't you mention this last night?"

Christopher's cheeks went pink. "I didn't want to make a big deal out of it in front of the guy. Besides, I didn't think you were going to end up skiing with him. I mean, of all people."

"This is insane," I said. "I just can't imagine—"

"You don't believe me?" Christopher demanded. "Because he—"

Suddenly he clamped up and sat back against the couch cushions again. I felt someone walk up behind me and knew it was Damon before he even said my name.

"Tess! You ready to go?" He glanced dismissively at Christopher. "What's up, man?"

Christopher said nothing. I couldn't believe this. I couldn't believe that I was finally going to ski a black diamond, and I was going up the mountain with a reckless jackass who had not only caused a serious injury, but seemed to have no remorse about it. He hadn't apologized to Christopher at karaoke last night. He'd barely said anything.

Was it possible Christopher had somehow misinterpreted what had happened on Christmas? Maybe this whole thing was just a misunderstanding and Damon was entirely innocent.

"Come on, Tess!" Lauren and Carina shouted from across the lobby, their voices echoing off the high ceilings.

I stood up slowly. If I stuck with my sister, I'd be okay. Besides, it wasn't like Damon was some psycho out to injure everyone on the mountain. If Lauren was right, and he really did like me, he wasn't about to hurt me. I just had to get through today, and then Christopher and I could talk more about this later.

"I guess I should . . . go," I said.

"Yeah. Uh . . . have fun," Christopher said.

"We will," Damon told him, draping his arm over my shoulder.

Christopher's jaw clenched, and my face burned. "I'll see you later," I promised Christopher. "Have a good day."

It felt like the lamest thing to say ever, but I couldn't think of anything else.

Christopher refused to look me in the eye, firing up his laptop and pretending to be riveted by whatever he was watching on his screen.

"Yeah," he said. "You too."

Damon turned and started to walk away, and I followed him slowly.

"And Tess," Christopher said, forcing me to turn back around. "Be careful," he added.

I headed for the door, wishing he hadn't sounded quite so ominous.

CHAPTER TWELVE

"I can't believe you've never skied a black diamond before. This is gonna be epic! Do you want me to ski behind you and take video?"

Damon hadn't stopped talking since we'd boarded the ski lift to the top of the slopes ten minutes earlier. So far I'd learned that he lived two towns over with Tarek and his parents—Damon's aunt and uncle—because his own parents were always traveling for work. He and Tarek went to the same high school and were even in the same grade, because they'd been born only three months apart. Both of them wanted to be traveling ski instructors once they graduated. The plan was to start out in Vermont and learn as much as they possibly could here before moving on to Colorado, where they had heard you could make a killing teaching wealthy people how to ski in Aspen or Vail.

"You only have to work like five hours a day, tops. And you're sitting pretty," he'd said. "I can spend the rest of my time skiing, playing video games, or just, like, napping. It's gonna be amazing."

Honestly, I thought it was cool that he had a life plan, and that he and his cousin wanted to stick together. My dad would have said that aspiring to work five hours a day wasn't very ambitious, but they were both working their butts off now at Evergreen Lodge, saving up enough money for their first apartment in Vermont. I admired all of it.

And I really couldn't imagine this smart, well-read person-with-a-plan could purposely run someone off a ski trail and into a tree. But did that mean I didn't believe Christopher? No. I *had* to believe Christopher. He was my friend. He was my . . . maybe more-than-friend. And whatever happened up there, I believed that *he* believed he was telling the truth.

Honestly, though, by the time we reached the top of the ski lift, I had no idea *what* to think.

Although, a tiny suspicion had worked its way into my mind. Maybe Christopher wasn't just upset that I was skiing with Damon. Maybe he was upset that I was skiing with *any* guy that wasn't him. Could he possibly be . . . jealous? But it wasn't as if I'd sought out Damon and made a plan to spend the day alone with him. He just happened to be along for the ride while I tried to eliminate another item from my to-do list. And, okay, he was hot and thought my singing had been amazing. (He must have been tone-deaf.) But that didn't mean Christopher had to be so surly. Except for the whole maybe-Damon-had-tried-to-kill-him thing.

Could he be jealous after knowing me for two days? The thought gave me butterflies in the pit of my stomach. It felt good to have someone jealous over me. I wished I'd spent a few more minutes talking to him this morning. I hated the way we'd left things.

"Are you telling me you can ski a black diamond while filming on your phone?" I asked Damon now, as our chair edged closer and closer to the drop-off point.

He laughed. "No way. Are you kidding? I've got a GoPro."

Out of his pocket he pulled a tiny little camera on a strap that he quickly secured to the crown of his head. I'd seen them now and then at skateboarding competitions, when skaters wanted to make first-person videos of their tricks.

"All right, then. Film away." The chair reached the top of the mountain, and we skied off, joining Lauren and Tarek, who were already waiting for us, their ski goggles pushed up on top of their helmets, the sun shining on their fresh faces. It was actually a perfect day for skiing. The wind was nonexistent and the sun was fairly strong, warming any exposed skin. It wasn't even that cold, even here at the top of the slope, where I usually found it to be freezing.

"All right, Tess. This is your deal. Do you want to do a few warm-up runs first, or do you want to just go for the black?" Tarek asked, adjusting his cowl-neck scarf.

"You told him?" I said to Lauren, irrationally irritated.

"What else was I going to talk about the whole ride up here?" She turned her palms up with her ski poles strapped to her wrists.

I groaned and skied away from them a bit, trying to remove myself from the center of attention. Lauren followed. "What's wrong?" she asked. "So Tarek knows you've never skied a black diamond. Isn't it safer if he knows to keep an eye out for you?"

"Yeah, I guess," I said, fiddling with my ski gloves. "I just . . . I don't know. Maybe I shouldn't go through with this."

I was starting to feel nervous now that we were up here. It had been almost a year since I'd even been on skis.

"Why *are* we going through with this, exactly?" Lauren asked again.

I took a breath and looked at her, trying to decide whether or not to take the plunge and tell her the truth. A truth that I could feel bubbling up in my throat even as we stood there. I squeezed my eyes shut and just let it out. "I made a bucket list."

"Are you dying?" she demanded, grabbing my wrist.

"What?" My eyes flew open. "No! Oh my God, no. If I were dying, do you really think this is how you'd find out?"

"Okay, fine. But don't freak me out like that." She put her hands to her head and straightened her goggles strap. "I almost had a heart attack."

"I'm touched," I said with a smile.

She grumbled. "Don't get all sappy on me now. Okay, so . . . what kind of bucket list?"

"It's ten things I have to do before the end of the year," I explained in a rush, trying to not give her the opportunity to interrupt and mock me. "It's so I can start the new year off right. I already completed four."

"What were they?" she asked. I glanced past her at the guys, who were busy taking pictures of one another doing silly ski poses.

"Fly a paper airplane for more than twenty seconds, wear heels in public, sing in public, and talk to a stranger." I ticked each item off on my fingers.

Lauren tipped her head back. "Oh, everything makes *so* much more sense now. And skiing a black diamond is on the list?"

"Yes."

"What else is on this list?" she asked, waggling her eyebrows.

"Get your mind out of the gutter," I said.

"Is smooching *Christopher* on this list?" she teased.

"No." I blushed furiously. "Christopher helped me *make* the list, so I couldn't exactly put that on there. I mean, I wouldn't have anyway, but still."

An odd heaviness settled inside my chest. It felt weird crossing something off my list without Christopher here to see it. Although, I guess he hadn't been around when I'd talked to Carina for the first time. Speaking of which . . . I glanced around and didn't see a bright pink jacket and helmet anywhere. Except for on the rather adorable five-year-old skiing past us for the green trail.

"Where's Carina?"

"Oh, she went inside to use the bathroom," Lauren said with a wave of her hand. "Okay, so this is a big deal. When Tess has a list, that list gets *done,* so you are *not* chickening out now. Besides, you've been talking about doing this for *years,* and every time we come here you invent some excuse. *It's too cold. I'm too tired. I have the flu—*"

"I *did* have the flu! I was puking my guts out, remember?"

"I'm just saying, now is your time, Tess. That's why you put it on your list. Because you knew it was your time. Don't blow it just because Christopher made you feel like crap."

I narrowed my eyes at her. I hadn't even told her what Christopher and I had talked about. How did she know, though, that he had so thoroughly gotten under my skin? Sometimes, I swear, Lauren had some sort of weird sisterly sixth sense that not only gave her an insane ability to annoy me, but also an insane ability to pump me up. I just wished she would use the latter more often. Should I tell her what he'd said about Damon? Maybe Tarek had been there with them. Maybe he had seen what had happened. But if he had, he hadn't told Lauren about it, or she definitely would have told me.

Carina skied over to us, stopping expertly and throwing up a wave of snow.

"Are you guys ready?" she asked.

Lauren raised her eyebrows at me. I clenched my jaw. My sister was right. Now was the time. And I wasn't going to let anyone—not Christopher or Damon or *anyone*—screw it up for me.

"Yes," I said, and snapped my goggles on. "Let's do it."

• • •

I stayed behind my sister, doing my best to follow her tracks as she skittered back and forth across the slope. Tarek and Damon were bringing up the rear for safety reasons. They didn't say that out loud, but I caught the look they exchanged with my sister before we started, and it was clear they were prepared to save me if I fell, or perform triage if I fell *bad*. I couldn't reconcile the guy who would literally get my back on the slopes with the guy Christopher had described to me, but I also couldn't think about that now. I had to concentrate on getting to the bottom in one piece.

Carina stuck to my side. I could tell she was a better skier than me, but she didn't try to get ahead of me or show off. It was like I had an entire entourage bent on getting me to the end of the trail safely.

Which was good, because for the first ten minutes, I was sure I was going to die. It might have been thirty seconds, actually. But it felt like ten minutes. Other skiers kept zipping past me down the mountain, coming so close I could feel the breeze of their momentum hitting me in the face. One guy got so near me I could smell his sunscreen. Couldn't they see I was in crisis mode over here?

But the longer I stayed on my feet, the more I began to relax. I started to feel the warmth of the sun on my face, alternating with the bitterness of the updraft as I flew downhill. I even let my leg muscles relax the tiniest bit, which helped me lean into turns a little more. This wasn't half bad, really. And in another ten minutes, it would be over. Whether I would be alive or dead when it *was* over was anyone's guess.

"How're you doing?" Carina yelled when we saw the marker indicating we were halfway down.

"Okay!" I called back, glancing over at her. Big mistake. My focus was broken. I lost my bearings and immediately felt my balance shift. My heart and stomach switched places as I started to veer off course.

"Lean right!" Damon shouted from behind me.

I did as directed, but I overcorrected, and my skis skidded out from under me.

"The other right!" Damon cried.

But it was too late. I was already on my back and sliding fast. One ski popped off, then the other. All I could think in my panic was *Did he do that on purpose? What the hell did he mean by "the other right"?* Tree branches and clouds zipped through my line of vision as I picked up speed. Oh my God, I was going to die. I was going to die I was going to die. Weirdly, it wasn't my life that flashed before my eyes, but Christopher, sitting on that couch in the lobby, looking adorable, laughing.

Christopher. Ugh. He was going to be so pissed at me if I didn't finish my list. So pissed that I didn't listen to him when he'd said that Damon was dangerous.

That was it. No dying today. Desperate, I grappled for handfuls of snow or rocks or anything that could slow me down, but it was no good. I was going to go off the side of the mountain. I could feel it. Any second and I'd be in free fall.

And then, I saw a zip of blue, and suddenly, I hit something. *Oof.* Hard, but not too hard. For a second I felt dizzy. Nothing moved other than a few wispy clouds high above. My breath was staggered and loud, but behind it I could hear birds chirping high in the trees and people whooping and calling on the slope. My face was raw, and ice particles dug into my cheeks, but I was alive.

I stared at the sky and breathed, afraid to move a single muscle.

"You're okay." It was Damon's voice. "You're okay."

I heard someone calling my name and realized it was my sister, so I sat up. She was climbing back up the mountain slowly, one difficult step at a time, her skis perpendicular to the slope.

"Tess! Are you all right?"

"I'm fine!" I glanced over and saw Damon sprawled next to me on his stomach, his skis and poles nowhere to be seen. "Did you just dive in front of me?"

He pushed himself up on his hands. The whole front of his ski jacket and pants were caked with snow. "Sort of? I didn't want you to hit that."

I looked left to see what he was pointing at. There was a huge wall of gray rock, covered in ice, about ten yards from where we were sitting. If I'd slid into that thing at the speed I'd been going, something would have gotten broken. An arm, a leg. Maybe my skull.

"Wow," I said, overwhelmed. "I . . . Thank you."

Damon grinned. "Anytime. I guess you could kind of say I'm your hero now."

I almost rolled my eyes, but stopped myself. Because it was basically true.

Tarek and Carina skied over to us just as Lauren finally arrived at my side. Tarek toted my skis under one arm. "Are you sure you're okay?" Lauren asked, lifting her goggles on top of her head. "That looked nasty."

"It was," I said. "But I'm okay. I think." I took a deep breath and slumped. "Remind me again why I did this?"

"Because it's awesome?" Tarek suggested.

Damon had shoved himself to his feet and reached out his arms to me. I took his hands, my ski poles still attached to my wrists, and let him haul me up. I dusted off the front of my snow pants while my sister whacked ice and snow off the back of my jacket. I could feel rope burns on my wrists, and there was snow down my back. I wondered if I'd discover any other random bruises or scrapes later. But for now, I was fine.

"Okay. But I never want to do it again," I said.

"Well, that's unfortunate," Carina said, biting her bottom lip. "Why?"

"Because we still have to get to the bottom of the mountain," Lauren answered.

"Oh." I looked down the slope, where skiers seemed to be dropping straight down over the next dip. "Crap."

• • •

A few minutes later, we were at the bottom. I saw the people up ahead of me slowing and sliding off toward the chair lift and whooped with joy. As the hill leveled out, I dug in and stopped myself, every muscle in my legs quivering, my entire body giddy with relief. I whipped off my helmet and goggles and tipped my face toward the sky.

"You made it!" Damon cheered, skiing right into me for a hug.

"I did!" I cheered back, just happy to be alive.

And then he took off his goggles and kissed me. It was a closed-mouthed celebratory kiss, but it lingered a second longer than it technically needed to. My heart pounded at the sensation of his well-ChapSticked lips on mine, his arms lightly around my waist. When he pulled back and smiled, my first and only thought was *I don't know his last name. Does this count?*

"Nicely done!" my sister congratulated me as she stopped right next to us. I couldn't tell if she was talking about the second half of my black diamond run, or the fact that Damon had just kissed me, but from the way she was looking at him, I had a feeling it was the latter.

"Thanks," I said, tucking my hair behind my ear and looking at the ground, sure I was blushing furiously. Hopefully I was already red from exertion and all the wind and ice burn, so no one would notice.

"We're having a staff party out at the barn later," Damon told us. "You guys should come."

"Oh, we'll be there," Lauren said, putting her arm around me. "We have to celebrate Tess's inaugural black diamond!"

Okay. That kiss definitely didn't count as *making out*. But if I went to this party later, maybe I'd get the chance to check that off my list. I looked up at Damon. He was smiling at me like he was thinking the same thing, and my heart fluttered with nerves. But it wasn't the good, crushy kind of nerves. It was just nerves.

I don't want *to make out with him,* I realized.

Because the only person in my heart and mind at that moment was Christopher.

• • •

TESS'S NEW YEAR'S BUCKET LIST

1. Make a paper airplane that actually flies (20 seconds at least) ✓
2. Sing in public ✓
3. Strike up a conversation with a stranger ✓
4. Wear high heels outside the house ✓
5. Make out with a guy whose last name I don't know (???)
6. TP someone's house
7. Get Adam Michel's autograph
8. Get a short, stylish haircut
9. Ski a black diamond slope ✓
10. Eat sushi

. . .

I was still breathless with adrenaline as we walked back into the lodge a couple of hours later. Carina and I had skied a few easier slopes while my sister stuck with the boys on the death trap mountain trails (as I had come to call them in my head). Once I'd managed to live through the black diamond experience, though, all the other trails seemed like cake walks, and I'd had a fun afternoon exerting myself and looking forward to seeing Christopher. Would it be weird to just throw myself into his arms and kiss him? Was that even something I could do?

I figured I'd know when I saw him. But first I had to ditch Damon and the rest of the group. I had a feeling that even laying eyes on Damon would keep Christopher from getting into any sort of kissing mood.

"What're you guys doing now?" Tarek asked as we walked into the lobby, the warm, cinnamon-scented air enveloping us. The sound system was still pumping in the Christmas carols, and right now it was a peppy rendition of "It's the Most Wonderful Time of the Year."

"I'm going to go see how my friend is doing," I said, gesturing toward the fireplace area. "He broke his leg a couple days ago and has to sit in the lobby all day. He must be bored out of his mind."

I watched Damon for a reaction as I said all of this, but he didn't flinch or even blink. If he had been involved in Christopher's accident, he was a really good actor.

"Okay, so, we'll see you later? At the party?" he said.

Was it just me, or was he giving me a *significant* look?

"I don't know. Maybe. I might have other plans," I said, feeling awkward.

Lauren barked a laugh. "What other plans? You literally never have plans."

I glared at her. Honestly. Could she *be* more humiliating? "That is one hundred percent untrue."

"Well, I'll be there," Carina said, breaking the tension as she glanced at her phone. "Meet back here at nine? Whoever's going?"

"Sounds like a plan!" Tarek said. He knocked Damon in the

chest with the back of his hand, and Damon backed away from me slowly.

"I hope you make it," he said to me earnestly.

"Um, yeah. Okay. I'll try."

Then he turned and followed his cousin out the door.

"Well, I need a long shower," my sister said, stretching her arms above her head. "See you later, Carina."

"Bye! Thanks for letting me tag along!" Carina gave us both a wave and headed off down the hallway at the back of the lobby—the one that led outside to the private cabins. She must have been staying in one of those with her father.

As soon as everyone was gone, I felt like a weight had lifted off my shoulders. It was nice to know—or suspect, anyway—that Damon was interested in me, but it also felt like a lot of pressure. Especially since I didn't really feel the same way. Yes, he was cute, but I didn't get the smooshy feeling around him that I got around Christopher.

Christopher.

My heart did a funny little pitter-pat thing as I pulled my ski hat from my head and tugged off my gloves. I held them all between my hands and pivoted on my heel, grinning as I crossed the lobby to find him.

Hey . . . we need to talk, I practiced.

No. That's what people said when they were about to break up.

How was your day?

Um, no. We weren't an old married couple.

Christopher, I'm totally into you.

Ugh. Okay, maybe the throwing myself into his arms option was the best plan.

I came around the corner by the fireplace, which was roaring with a perfect fire, as always, and stopped in my tracks.

There was a girl sitting in my chair. A girl who was not me. And the not-me girl was talking to Christopher. Making him laugh. In *my* chair. So apparently he wasn't bored out of his mind.

"No way!" Christopher exclaimed, literally slapping his knee. "There's no way that actually happened."

"I swear it's true!" the girl replied in a high, nasally voice. "He had third-degree burns *inside his nostrils.*"

Okay, ew. What the heck were they even talking about? And why were third-degree burns funny? In the midst of his latest bout of uncontrollable laughter, Christopher happened to glance up and spot me hovering. His face fell, and he looked at my hands, which I realized suddenly were clutching my hat and gloves in front of my chest as if in prayer. I dropped my arms immediately.

"Oh," he said coolly. "Hi, Tess."

The girl turned around to look at me. She was, annoyingly, pretty. She had big brown eyes and ridiculously long lashes, plus that kind of curly hair that bounces whenever the person who has it moves. She wore a low-cut lavender T-shirt and a white puffer vest. A gold nameplate necklace that read *Kacey* dangled just above her cleavage.

"Hi!" she said, though her confused eyes betrayed her peppy greeting. "I'm Kacey!"

"Tess," I said. "Nice to meet you." I glanced over at Christopher, who seemed very interested in the floral pattern embroidered on the back of the couch. He was picking at a tiny string with his thumbnail, avoiding eye contact with both of us. "Are you staying at the lodge?" I asked, mostly to fill the awkward silence.

"Yeah, I just got here." Kacey looked down at her phone. "Oh, dang. I gotta go. My mom wants me to watch my little brother while she goes to the spa." Kacey got up and shoved her device into the back pocket of her tight jeans. "I'll see you later?" she said to Christopher.

"Oh, definitely," he replied. "You know where to find me."

That stung. This was where *I* knew to find him. Not some random girl with bouncy hair.

"Nice to meet you, Tess," she said. Then she twiddled her fingers at Christopher and strode away. Even after she was gone, Christopher still refused to look at me.

"Well. She seemed nice," I said tersely.

"Why do you have to say it like that?" he snapped. "She *is* nice."

"I'm sure she is." What was I saying? Why was I saying it? My skin felt hot all over and my eyes prickled with frustrated tears.

"Well, I'm glad to see you survived skiing with Damon," Christopher said. "I guess when he wants to hook up with someone, he's a little more careful on the slopes."

Oh. My. God. Did he actually just say that to me? I mean, Damon did kiss me, but still. Christopher didn't know that.

"He wasn't just careful," I told him hotly. "He actually saved my life."

Christopher scoffed. "Yeah, right."

"He did! I totally decked up there and was about to slide face-first into a wall of rock, but he threw himself in front of me," I said.

"Whoa, really?" Christopher's expression shifted to one of concern. "Tess, are you okay?"

"Yes, I'm fine," I said, taking a deep, shaky breath. "But only thanks to Damon."

I just wanted him to back off the guy. Maybe Damon *had* done something stupid when he was skiing with Christopher, but he wasn't all bad. Clearly. Besides, I wanted to move on with the conversation, which was so not going the way I'd daydreamed it would go.

"He was probably just trying to get in good with Loretta so he wouldn't get fired," Christopher muttered.

"Wait . . . what? Is he getting fired?"

Christopher looked away. "No. I don't . . . Forget I said anything."

"No, tell me," I said, suddenly remembering the conversation we'd had about getting whoever did this fired. "Christopher, what's going on?"

He huffed a sigh, clearly uncomfortable. "My parents . . . they're pretty pissed about what happened. They demanded Loretta fire Damon."

I blinked, confused. Normally, my grandmother toed the "the customer is always right" line pretty closely. If someone demanded an employee be fired, especially after an egregious offense, she normally listened. It's not like I wanted Damon to lose his job, but I knew how Loretta would see it. He was just another dude serving coffee, and there were always local kids lined up to take jobs here. Although, she'd probably never used the word "dude" in her life.

"So . . . why hasn't she?" I asked.

"Because her lawyers told her not to, apparently," Christopher said. "They said it would be like admitting guilt." He shot me a fleeting look and turned even redder. "I don't know the details. My parents don't tell me everything, so you'd have to ask her. I probably shouldn't even be talking to you about this. They'd probably say I was sharing confidential information or something."

My stomach was doing this awful clenching and unclenching

thing that I really did not like. "I'm sorry . . . *sharing confidential information?*" When had this become an episode of *Law & Order?* "Christopher, why are there lawyers involved?"

"Can we talk about something else?" Christopher asked, shifting in his seat. "So, you did it, huh? You skied a black diamond. Have you checked it off your list yet?" He was forcing this odd, fake-chipper voice, and it just made me feel worse.

"Christopher, are you . . . are you suing my grandmother?"

"No! No. We're just . . . suing the resort."

"That's the same thing!" I cried.

"No, it's not. The resort is a company. We're suing the company."

"My *family's* company!" I replied, maybe a touch too loudly. A few people relaxing in the lobby turned to look, and my throat tightened. "This place could go bankrupt," I said, lowering my voice. "My grandmother would lose everything."

"Tess, calm down. It's not like this was my decision," he said. "It was my parents'. And there's no talking them out of something once they decide to do it."

"You have to tell them Damon didn't do anything," I said.

He went very still. "But Damon *did* do something. He ran me off the trail. He even laughed about it."

"How do you know it wasn't just a reaction to seeing you fall? I mean, not the greatest reaction, but still. Some people automatically laugh in the face of tragedy, you know," I informed him. "How do you know for sure you wouldn't have broken your leg anyway?"

"Oh my God," Christopher said. "You really don't believe me."

My face was burning and I was starting to truly sweat. "And you want to put my grandmother out on the street."

"That's a little dramatic, Tess."

"No, it's not! It's the truth. This place is all she has. These people are her family." I threw out my arms as if to encompass the entire resort. "This is *my* family."

"Wow." Christopher's face had gone stony. "It's all about you, isn't it?"

"What's that supposed to mean?"

He pushed his hands into the couch at his sides and shoved himself up straighter. "My leg is broken, Tess. I'm in constant pain over here. I'm going to miss an entire season of basketball. But do you even care? No. It's all about you and your parents and your list and your grandmother's hotel. Well, guess what? One of her employees injured me. On purpose. And the reality is that the hotel is liable. And instead of caring about any of that, you're running out the front door to go skiing with the guy who did this to me!"

"You were the one who told me I had to start doing more things for myself. Isn't that how this whole thing got started?" I shouted, rousing an older couple from a couch nearby. "And now you're calling me *selfish*? What do you want from me, Christopher?"

"Nothing," he said flatly, his jaw clenched. "Okay, Tess? I want nothing from you."

My heart sunk all the way into my frostbitten toes. I couldn't believe that, mere minutes ago, I'd been daydreaming about kissing this guy. "Fine," I replied. "Then I guess I'll just go."

And then, I did.

I went right to Loretta's office. Her assistant, Frank, looked stressed out when I walked in, but he managed a smile. The door behind him—the one that led to Loretta's room—was closed.

"Hi, Tess," he said. "She's on the phone right now, but I'll let her know you're here."

"Thanks."

He typed something quickly into his computer, and it dinged a second later.

"She says to send you right in."

My whole body was jangling with nerves as I pushed open the door. Loretta stood up from behind her desk, hanging up her phone as she did. I was still trying to figure out exactly what to say, when she spoke first.

"Did you just get into an altercation in the lobby?"

Her voice was tense, and it wasn't until I heard it that I noticed her whole face was red.

"How did you—"

"I have staff who tend to alert me to these sorts of things," she reminded me. "This isn't like you, Tess. First the incident at the pool and now this. You know better. When you're here, you're a representative of this family, of this resort. You have to be on your best behavior."

I was so taken aback I didn't know what to say. Here I'd been about to ask her about the lawsuit—to try to help—and she was attacking me.

"Did they tell you who I was arguing with?" I asked.

"That's hardly the point, Tess."

"No, actually, it *is* the point," I told her, shaking from the effort of having yet another argument. She was right. This wasn't like me. And I didn't like it. "I was arguing with Christopher Callahan. You know, the person whose family is suing Evergreen Lodge?"

Loretta paled. "How do you know about that?"

"Because he told me!" I cried. "Why didn't *you* tell me?"

Her lips twitched, and she stood completely still. "Because it is none of your concern."

"How is it not my concern?" I demanded. "You knew I was

hanging out with him. You could have told me. Do you think I don't care about this place? Maybe I can help. Maybe I can—"

Loretta barked a laugh. A not-at-all-kind laugh. "Tess, I appreciate that you feel passionate about this, but you need to stay out of it. You and Christopher shouldn't even be talking about this."

"Why not?" I asked.

"Because you are a minor," she shot back. "And so is he. And there are a hundred nuances involved in this matter that you couldn't possibly understand. This is the type of thing that needs to be left to the grown-ups."

My jaw dropped open, but no sound came out. I felt so insulted I wanted to scream.

"Now go to your room," she said, dismissing me like I wasn't just a child, but a small one. A child she couldn't bear to be around any longer. "And don't talk to that boy about this again, do you understand?"

I didn't move. I still couldn't speak.

"I said, do you understand?" she said slowly.

"I understand," I whispered.

Chapter Thirteen

I slammed the door to our room so hard, the wall sconces rattled. Lauren was still in the shower—I could hear the water running and her off-key singing echoing off the walls. I let out a groan and paced over to the window, stripping out of my ski jacket and sweatshirt and kicking off my boots. The cool air hit my sweaty skin, and I immediately shivered, but felt maybe one percent better.

I couldn't believe Loretta had spoken to me that way. I mean, she'd never been the warmest person, but for half a second there she'd looked like a villain out of some horrible kids' cartoon. Didn't she understand I just wanted to help? And she'd dismissed me like I was nothing. I hadn't even had the chance to ask her how much money they were suing for. If it could ruin the business. And had she talked to my father about it? Had she asked for his advice?

Honestly, I was still having a hard time wrapping my brain around the fact that it was even happening. Christopher's family was suing the resort. Okay, yes, businesses got sued every day. My father was legal counsel for a resort chain, so I knew. I knew the kinds of things people would get litigious about. They sued over food poisoning. Over falling down in the lobby while the floor was being mopped. Over there being no gluten-free options on a menu. Sure, someone might sue over an employee injuring their son. But this was *my* family. And it was my friend who was suing us.

At least, I'd thought Christopher was my friend. Couldn't he have told me about this the second he found out Loretta was my grandmother? *Shouldn't* he have? Maybe I could have talked him out of it. Or at least talked to Damon and tried to figure out what had actually happened. Maybe it was just a misunderstanding, and I could have helped figure it out.

I sat down on the bed and took a deep breath. But then, everything else came rushing back at me. Like that girl, Kacey, for starters. Did Christopher really like her? What had they talked about while I was up on the mountain? Had they talked about me and my list? Had they *laughed* about it? And also, he seemed so pissed off that I'd gone skiing without him. Or was it really the fact that I'd gone skiing *with* Damon? Or was it both? Because if Christopher had wanted to be at my side for every single thing I accomplished on my list, then he should have spoken up when I'd added the black diamond slope the other night. I could have thought of something else. Something we could do together.

But honestly, was it really my responsibility to keep him entertained all day? Whether or not Damon had been involved, Christopher had a broken leg. There was no getting around that. He would have been stuck in that lobby whether Lauren and I had ever shown up here or not. He had no right to blame me for wanting to get out of the lodge for a bit and have a little fun. I mean, hello? This was my vacation.

The second that thought hit me, I stopped pacing. Because it didn't sound like me at all. My whole intention when I'd arrived here was to spend the entire week on my butt reading books and watching videos. If I was being honest, that's what I would have done if not for Christopher suggesting I get out of my comfort zone. If not for his help making the list.

Why did everything have to be so complicated all of a sudden?

I groaned again and flopped back on my bed. My phone jutted into my hip, and I pulled it out. Damon had sent the video of me skiing the black diamond, which there was no way I could watch right now. I wasn't sure I could take the humiliation of watching myself fall on my butt. There were also half a dozen texts from my dad, asking what we were up to and requesting photos. He'd also sent me a picture of a misshapen tomato that looked like a heart that made me smile. I felt like I'd been neglecting him, so I sent him a couple of skiing pics Carina and I had taken. A text popped back almost immediately.

Who's the girl?
New friend. I skied a black diamond today.
No way! Congrats! So proud. And I'm glad you're making new friends. No boys though right?

I sighed and rolled my eyes.

Yes there are boys here. It's not Mars.
LOL but not a particular boy?

I hesitated for half a second. Did he know about Christopher somehow? Had Lauren clued him in? Doubtful. She wasn't really speaking to our father at the moment, just like I wasn't really speaking to our mom. Maybe Loretta had called him and told him about the paper airplane–flying incident? That I was flirting with the kid whose family was suing the resort? I blushed just thinking about that moment Loretta had interrupted, and irritation twisted my gut. Was that really just yesterday that I had felt so close to Christopher? That we'd almost kissed?

> **There is one guy. Christopher. But he's mad at me.**
> Wait. You already met a guy who is already mad at you? That's fast.

I laughed sadly.

> **He's pissed because I left him alone all day to go skiing. I think.**

I didn't want to be the one to tell him about the lawsuit if he didn't already know. That would just set him off and he'd call Loretta and then she'd get mad at me. Unless she *had* already told him. And if she had, then I didn't want to get in the middle of it. But I doubted it. Loretta seemed to keep the business of Evergreen Lodge far out of my father's orbit, for some reason. I never fully understood why. My dad texted back.

> Why didn't he go with you?
> **He has a broken leg.**
> Oh. Bummer. Did you go with Lauren?
> **Yes and some other people. Two other guys and Carina from the pics.**
> Cute guys???

DAD!
Well I'm just saying maybe he's jealous.

My skin burned. It definitely seemed like Christopher might be jealous of Damon, but somehow my dad saying it made it seem even more absurd than it already did. Back home, no boys liked me. Well, except that blip with Frankie. Not counting that, I had to go all the way back to eighth grade when Ryan Della Torre had kissed me backstage at the fall musical and told me he liked my hair. It just wasn't possible that, after being here for three days, I had two boys crushing on me.

I don't know. I guess they're cute.
That's it then. This Christopher guy likes you back,
Tater. Just deal with it.

I snorted a laugh. Sometimes talking to my dad was more like talking to a girlfriend. But I really had to get him to stop calling me Tater. That had been my nickname ever since I was three and I'd apparently spent six months refusing to eat anything other than tater tots.

Okay, maybe. But then what do I do?

There was a long pause, and for a second I thought I might have lost my dad's attention, but then the three scrolling dots appeared.

Text him. See if he wants to hang out. It will make him
feel better if he gets to spend some time with you.

It was a simple answer. Because my dad didn't know about the added layer of the lawsuit. I tried to see it from my father's point of view—to set aside the fact that Christopher's parents were attacking my grandmother. The last thing Christopher had said to me was that he didn't want anything from me. And now I was supposed to text him and invite him . . . to do what, exactly? Go to the staff party with me? The one Damon had invited me to? I didn't think that would go over well.

OK. I'll try.

I texted this mostly to make my dad think he'd given me good advice. Really, I wasn't sure what I was going to do.

OK good luck! And tell your sister to text me. Or call me. Either one.
I will.

I put the phone down and stared at the ceiling. All the anger had seeped out of me, leaving me feeling tired and lonely. The water finally turned off inside the bathroom, and I glanced at the time. Wow. Lauren had been serious when she'd said she was going to take a long shower. Suddenly, I could feel the dried sweat sticking my hair to the back of my neck, and I shivered. Hopefully she didn't use all the hot water.

A couple minutes later, my sister came out of the bathroom all bundled up in an Evergreen Lodge robe and a towel around her head, releasing a cloud of steam.

"Hey," she said. "How's it going?"

I had so much to tell her. So much had happened between

when she'd left me in the lobby and now. But I didn't have the energy for it at the moment. All I could think about was getting in the shower and cleaning the last thirty minutes off of me.

"Fine." I shoved myself up. "Dad wants you to call him. I'm going to take a shower."

I heard her grumbling as I closed the door behind me. Standing in the center of her residual steam, I quickly texted Christopher, before I could double-think it.

That conversation did not go well. Truce?

I stared at my phone, holding my breath. Ten seconds. Twenty. Nothing. Maybe he wasn't looking at his phone. I tried another tactic.

Sorry I yelled. I was just shocked.

Still nothing. I added:

Can we talk? Are you still in the lobby?

This time I waited a full two minutes, just willing the scrolling dots to appear. But there was still no response. I slapped the phone down on the counter, stripped out of my clothes, and got in the shower. Maybe by the time I was all cleaned up and warm, he would have texted back. But when I emerged from the shower a few minutes later and grabbed my phone, my heart all but died.

Not a single message in reply.

I bit my bottom lip. Should I try another text? What would I even say? No. I couldn't do it. If he wanted to reply to me, he would. I mean, he was the one whose family was trying to take down my family. Shouldn't he be the one apologizing? Shouldn't he have reached out first? Suddenly, I felt angry all over again and turned off my phone completely. Maybe we both needed the night to cool off.

Tomorrow was a totally new day.

...

DECEMBER 30

I woke up so early the next morning, the light coming through the crack between the curtains was still pinkish gray. Lauren had come back so late, I'd barely registered it. That staff party must have been one for the ages. I wondered if Damon had been disappointed when I didn't show up. If Lauren and Carina had bonded and were now BFFs. Probably. Lauren had a way of becoming BFFs with everyone she met. But at the moment, I didn't really care. I needed to find Christopher. I needed to make everything that had gone wrong between us, right. I just really hoped he felt the same way.

I took a quick shower, pulled my hair up in a wet bun, and dressed in my favorite buffalo plaid shirt, cozy white sweater, and comfy gray leggings. It was not only a cute outfit, but functional if I was going to spend the morning cozied up by the fire, figuring out the next move on my list with Christopher, like I hoped. Maybe, if we made up, I could even talk to his parents. Get them to see that there were real people behind this company they were suing. The very idea terrified me, but I'd do it if I could. Evergreen Lodge meant a lot to my family. It meant a lot to me.

I grabbed my backpack with the list inside and slipped out, noticing that Lauren hadn't even changed out of her clothes before passing out on top of her comforter. I rolled my eyes and closed the door quietly behind me.

Downstairs, the lodge had that just-waking-up feeling. The really dedicated ski bums sipped coffee in the lounge, surrounded by their gear, ready to hit the slopes before anyone else could even contemplate breakfast. People spoke in hushed tones, respectful of the early hour, and the Christmas music could be easily heard over the quiet conversations. As I crossed the lobby, a man belly-laughed, and the sound was so startling that everyone in sight looked up. I smiled and headed for the fireplace. But Christopher wasn't there.

Not shocking, I supposed, since it was so early, but I still felt a sinking disappointment in my gut. I decided to hang out on his couch and wait, figuring he'd be along soon. He'd mentioned that he was more of a morning person than a night person, and breakfast was his favorite meal of the day. It wouldn't be long before his stomach sent him in search of French toast. I pulled out my book and settled in to read.

A half hour went by. Then another. The lobby grew louder and more crowded around me as families headed for breakfast or out to the slopes or ordered cars to take them into town for the day. Every now and then I glanced up and scanned the room, just in case Christopher had spotted me and decided to camp out somewhere else. I hoped he wouldn't do that, but you never knew. After an hour and a half had gone by, I was so hungry I couldn't ignore it anymore. I shoved my book back into my bag and went to the Antelope Room for breakfast. Maybe Christopher had gone straight to the buffet instead of stopping off in the lobby.

The dining room was crowded. I saw Carina sitting alone with her book at a far table, completely absorbed by the story, but no sign of Christopher. Or Loretta for that matter. I had this odd ominous feeling. Like I was missing something. Whatever it was, I didn't like it. What if Loretta was already in some meeting with her lawyers? Or locked in a heated battle with Christopher's parents in one of the conference rooms? I joined the line for pancakes, but kept one eye on the door. If I could just *see* Christopher, I knew I'd feel better. Instead, I saw his parents.

For a minute, I just watched the Callahans, trying to figure out what to do and get up the guts to do it. Christopher's dad looked a lot like Christopher, except his blond hair was slicked back from his face, and he had a more distinguished air about him. His mom wore slacks and a cashmere cardigan, her light brown hair cut to chin length and not a hair out of place. They walked over to the bar where they served coffee and espresso, the dad's hand on the small of the mom's back. Watching them made me feel hot all over. These were the people who were going after Loretta, after the Lodge, after my family. Why couldn't they just drop it? Let everyone move on with their lives? Yes, Christopher had been hurt, and that was awful, but everyone got hurt once in a while. My parents hadn't sued the company running the skateboarding competition when *I'd* broken *my* ankle.

I glanced behind the Callahans, figuring Christopher would be bringing up the rear on his crutches, but he didn't appear. A few more families and groups streamed through the doors, but no Christopher.

My heart began to pound uncomfortably. Where was he? I looked at his parents, who were now chatting while the woman behind the counter made their coffee drinks. I could just ask them. But that would be intrusive. And odd. I'd only ever met his mother once, briefly. And they looked so . . . I don't know, formal. For-bidding? Like people who didn't want to be bothered by other people. Especially by the granddaughter of the hotel owner they were suing.

Also, I was so bad at talking to strangers.

But this was an emergency.

Sort of.

I was almost at the front of the line. I could just grab a plate full of pancakes and retreat to Carina's corner and be done with it. But no. This was too important. It was time to be brave. I'd talked to Carina, and that had turned out fine. I could talk to these people, too.

Before I knew what was happening, I had stepped away from the carb line and approached. The couple was just picking up their tiny espresso cups and turning around when I stepped in front of them. Christopher's mother let out a little "oh" and almost spilled her coffee.

Of course.

"Oh! Sorry! I didn't mean to. . . . Sorry," I said.

She narrowed her eyes at me like maybe she was trying to remember where she'd seen me before. I wanted to die right there.

"Can we help you with something?" Christopher's father said.

Yes, you can drop your lawsuit and go back to Princeton already, I thought. *But maybe leave your son behind so we can make up?*

"Yeah, I'm just . . . sorry," I said. "I was looking for Christo-pher?"

Sheesh. How many times could someone say *sorry* in the span of ten seconds? I sounded like I hadn't woken up yet.

"Christopher?" his dad said, as if he'd never heard the name before.

Wait. Did I have the wrong couple? Oh God, I really was going to die.

"Oh, right! You're that girl he was talking to! Jess!"

"Tess," I said, and blushed.

"Right. Tess." She gave a tight smile. "Richard, this is Tess Sachs. Granddaughter of Loretta Sachs?"

He stiffened up so quickly I was surprised he didn't drop his coffee. Clearly he didn't want to be around anyone with the last name Sachs.

"I'm afraid Christopher's not here any longer," he said tersely. "He went to his cousins' house."

"Oh. Okay." I almost backed off, but somehow held my ground. "Sorry," I said again. "For the day?"

"For the rest of break," his mother replied in a kinder tone than his father had managed. "He was just so bored sitting on that couch all day. Not that I could blame him. It must have been torture for him watching people coming and going from the slopes all day and to be stuck there with nothing to do and no one to talk to."

My face burned even hotter, and I felt like crying. He had *me* to talk to.

"So . . . wait. You mean he's not coming back?" I asked.

"No. We're going to pick him up there the day after New Year's and fly home," his mother said, and gave me a sympathetic frown. "I'm sorry he didn't let you know."

"Oh. No. It's fine. We weren't. I mean, I didn't—"

Christopher's father glanced at his watch. "We should go, Maggie. We have that . . . call we need to be on."

He glanced at me out of the corner of his eye as he said this, and I knew he was taking a call with their lawyers. Suddenly I wanted to grab that stupid little coffee cup out of his hand and throw whatever was left in it right in his face.

But I didn't.

"Well. It was nice seeing you, Jess," Christopher's mother said.

His dad gave me a curt nod, and then they walked away.

I just stood there, staring at the spot where they'd been seconds before, trying not to burst into tears. Christopher was gone. He'd just up and left. Had he even gotten the texts I'd sent last night? Did it mean nothing to him that I'd reached out? That *I'd* apologized? Was he that angry? Did he believe in this lawsuit so much that he couldn't even acknowledge me? Apparently that was his plan. And now I was never going to see him again.

All I'd been to him was a distraction, and not even a very good one.

CHAPTER FOURTEEN

When I got back to our room, Lauren was gone. Bed unmade. Clothes everywhere. Good. I didn't want her here. I didn't want anyone anywhere near me. I flung myself onto my bed on my back, tears leaking out the corners of my eyes and pooling in my ears. I wasn't sobbing, exactly, but I couldn't stop the tears from quietly flowing. I couldn't believe he'd just left without saying goodbye. Without saying *anything*. I checked my phone just to make triple-sure, and the only text was from Carina.

Are you okay? I just saw you run out of the restaurant.

I thought about texting back, but what was I supposed to say? I barely knew her. Confessing that I was broken up about the fact that a guy I'd known for three days had bailed on me just felt so loser-y I could cry. Except I was already crying. I put the phone facedown on the bedside table and took deep breaths instead.

Try to put yourself in his place, I told myself. Yes, we'd been hanging out a lot over the last couple of days, but what about all the hours I wasn't there with him? I'm not saying I'm the most entertaining person on the planet, but what was he doing when I wasn't there? Watching videos until his eyes dried out? Texting with friends who were probably doing all kinds of fun things on their winter breaks? Maybe at his cousins' he'd have more to do. People to play video games with. An aunt and/or uncle who could take him out to the movies or the mall or somewhere other than a couch in the middle of a hotel lobby.

I couldn't blame him. My list, I'd thought, had been a fun distraction, but that was really just about me. Selfish old me. My heart squeezed when I thought of our argument the night before. Texting clearly wasn't working. I could just call him. See how he was doing. Say I was sorry for . . . what? Making him jealous with Damon? I wasn't even a hundred percent sure he *was* jealous. I mean, if he really liked me enough to get envious about a couple of hours on the slopes—most of which I didn't even spend with Damon, by the way, not that he'd given me a chance to tell him that—then wouldn't he still be here?

But maybe his leaving had nothing to do with any of this. Maybe he was just pissed off that I didn't understand why his family was suing my family. Maybe that was too much for us to get over. I had to talk to Loretta. I had to find out what was actually going on. I had to *make* her talk to me about it.

I lifted my phone again, and it rang. I was so startled I almost dropped it, but instead I hit *Accept*.

I didn't even have a chance to see who was calling. Maybe it was him?

"Hello?" I said.

"Tess! Hi, honey! How are you?"

My stomach clenched. It was my mother.

"Oh. Hi, Mom."

There was a pause. Clearly she could tell how not-psyched I was to talk to her.

"Is everything okay?" she asked gently.

No. Everything was not okay. And even though I was still mad at her, hearing her ask me that in her mom-voice got to me. Before I knew what was happening, I started to spill.

"I think I messed something up, and I don't know how to fix it," I said, my voice, annoyingly, cracking.

She took a deep breath, and I could just imagine her settling into her favorite chair by the window with a cup of tea. "Tell me what it is and we'll figure it out."

So I did. I told her everything. Well, not about the lawsuit, because I knew in the depths of my soul that Loretta wouldn't want me talking about it. But everything that had to do with me. How I felt like I was always doing things for other people, but never anything for myself. How I wanted to try new things and stop being so nervous all the time. Stop being the good girl— "Sorry, Mom"—all the time. She laughed at that. "No apologies necessary."

And then I told her about Christopher and how he'd helped me write, and laminate, and get started on completing the list.

"But then yesterday I went with Lauren and some other people to go ski the black diamond, and when I got back he was flirting with some other girl and he was so mad at me," I said. "Like I'd betrayed him somehow."

"But it's not like he could have gone skiing with all of you. His leg is broken," my mother said indignantly.

"Yes! Thank you! That's what I said!" I felt a little giddy over vibing with my mother. It had been a long time since we'd had a conversation like this. One that wasn't all tangled up with negative emotions about her and my dad breaking up. Maybe my parents had done the right thing sending me and Lauren away for the week. Maybe being physically farther apart was somehow bringing us closer.

"Anyway, I saw his parents this morning, and they said he'd left. He's going to spend the rest of his break at his cousins' house," I finished, staring up at the ceiling. I had to bite the inside of my cheek to keep from telling her about the lawsuit, and how that complicated everything. "So . . . so much for that."

"You don't think it's because of you, do you, honey?" my mom asked.

"I don't know. I mean, we have this big fight and then he's gone? If it's not about me, it seems kind of like a big coincidence."

"Well, I have to say I like the sound of this list," my mom told me. "You *should* get out of your comfort zone every once in a while."

I rolled my eyes, so not surprised that she liked the idea of the list. My mother was always after me to be more adventurous. To try out for the soccer team or go out for the school play. To meet new people. To be more like Lauren. Even to get back on my skateboard. Is that all my list was to her? A sign that I was going to become more like her favorite daughter? I bet she was psyched about that.

"Whatever happens with Christopher, you should keep chipping away at your list," she told me. "Don't let some boy and what he wants or doesn't want derail you from living your life."

Her voice sounded oddly bitter as she said this, and her words seemed to hang in the air around me. My fingers and toes tingled, and not in a good way. I clutched the phone a bit tighter, waiting for her to break the silence that had suddenly descended. When she didn't, I asked, in a small voice, "Mom . . . is that how you feel about Dad? Do you feel like he derailed your life?"

Please say no, I thought. Because if that's what she thought, didn't that mean that Lauren and I were part of that . . . derailment? That we were the result of some train wreck?

I knew my mom had moved away from her family and given up her job when my dad had been moved by the company to Philadelphia, right around when Lauren was born. She'd been working as a low-level assistant at some fashion company in New York that no longer even existed. But had she had dreams of a career in fashion? Did she regret letting my dad's job take over their lives?

How had I never asked her about any of this before? Suddenly I felt both very selfish and very scared. What if my mom hated our life together, and that's why she was breaking it all up?

"It's more complicated than that, Tess," she said finally. "Your dad and I . . . we both made decisions, apart and together, that got us to where we are. But I do sometimes wish that I'd spoken up for myself more when I was younger. That I'd understood that the things I wanted weren't frivolous or less important." She took a breath. "Tess, the things you want . . . they matter. They matter more than you know. So I say finish this list. Prove to yourself that you can do it. It could change everything."

I sat up straight on the bed, a steely resolve coming over me. She was right. This wasn't about Christopher. It was about me. Even if that did sound selfish. I had to finish my list. And I only had a day and a half to do it.

"Okay, Mom. I'll do my best."

···

There was one item on my list that had to happen today. Get Adam Michel's autograph. His book signing was at The Little Bookshop in town at two o'clock, and it was already pushing noon. I needed to find a way to get into town ASAP. If I knew Adam Michel's fans, and I was pretty sure I knew them well, as I'd been one of them almost my entire life, I knew they were already lined up to meet him. I texted Lauren.

WHERE ARE YOU? I need a ride into town.

Then I paced the room for ten minutes waiting for her to respond. No dice. I thought about going to find Loretta. But she'd been so pissed at me yesterday and, to be honest, I was still pissed at her for treating me like a baby. Besides, I was sure she was insanely busy, either dealing with lawyers or even just getting the staff ready for tomorrow night's New Year's Eve celebrations. I didn't want to bother her.

I glanced at the calendar she'd left for us on our first day here. There was a gingerbread house competition today, and it was marked as mandatory on our schedules. I paused, wondering if Lauren had any intention of showing up for that.

The thought made me laugh out loud.

I looked at my phone again. The last text I had was from Carina. I didn't think she was old enough to drive, but however I got to town, I was going to need a wingman. There was no way I was going to get up the guts to talk to Adam Michel on my own. Besides, if there was a long line to get my book signed, I'd need someone to talk to. I texted her back.

Hey! I'm fine. Where are you?

She wrote back right away.

Cafe. Reading.
Be right there.

I grabbed my backpack and headed back downstairs. Carina was sitting in one of the deep chairs by the window at the Best Bean, her feet up on the coffee table in front of her. I glanced over at the counter and was relieved to see that Damon wasn't working. I didn't want to get into last night's party and why I wasn't there. And I definitely didn't want to talk about Christopher or whether Damon was worried about losing his job.

"Hey!" Carina said, closing her book as I arrived. "What's up?"

"What are you doing today?" I asked.

"Not much. Why?"

"I need to go get Adam Michel's autograph. Do you want to come?"

"Adam Michel?" She seemed to freeze. Her hand went to her book, which she'd laid aside on the chair, and she clutched it almost like it was a security blanket. "What do you mean you *need* to get his autograph?" she said. "Why are you asking *me*?"

I sat down in the chair across from hers and opened my backpack. "Okay, this is going to sound crazy, but I made a list of ten things I have to do before the new year, and getting Adam Michel's autograph is on it. My sister found out he's going to be signing copies of his new autobiography in town today, and so I need to go."

I pulled out the laminated list and handed it over to her.

"Tess's New Year's Bucket List," she read, then gasped and looked at me. "You're not dying, are you?"

"No!" I said with a laugh. "Nothing like that."

Carina narrowed her eyes as she scanned the ten items and the various check marks. I felt like I was completely exposed, suddenly. Like she was either going to laugh at me for being such a dork or tell me I was insane. But instead, she lay the list down on her lap and looked at me.

"There's a date on this. You made it a couple of days before we met."

"Yeah." I felt a beat of apprehension. Why was she being so weird about this?

"So . . . you really don't know who I am?"

"I . . . what? Who are you?"

Carina smiled slowly, and her smile reminded me of the Cheshire Cat from *Alice in Wonderland*. Disturbing, but also intriguing. "Oh, this is going to be *such* fun."

• • •

Ten minutes later, Carina and I were in a sleek black car being whisked into town by someone named Phil, who kept calling her *Miss*. I felt a little bit like I'd just stepped into a movie and was either going to be kidnapped and held for ransom on a speeding train somewhere, or taken to the nearest posh city for a ridiculous makeover. Whenever I tried to ask Carina a question, she changed the subject, and before I knew it, we were pulling up in front of The Little Bookshop, where there was—as predicted—a line of rabid fans three deep and two blocks long waiting outside in the frigid cold. Half of them were wearing Adam Michel tour T-shirts, or had their hair teased and spiked up in Adam's preferred style. I suddenly felt kind of lame in my favorite comfy outfit.

"Is this all right, Miss?" Phil asked.

"This is perfect, Phil, thanks." Carina texted rapidly on her phone as I stared out the window.

"Ugh, it's too late," I said. "There's no way I'm ever getting to the front of this line. I bet these people got here at ten this morning."

"Some of them actually camped overnight," Carina said. She glanced at her phone as a text came in. "Okay. Let's go. Phil, we'll be back in, like, ten minutes unless I text you."

"Sounds good, Miss. I'll just circle the block for a bit."

"Ten minutes?" I said. Was she out of her mind? Did she not *see* the line? "What're you—"

But Carina had already opened the door of the car. Everyone on line near us turned to look, as if expecting someone famous to be stepping out, and a few of them actually did gasp when they saw us. What the heck was happening? Carina slipped on a pair of sunglasses and looked at the open door, where the line was snaking through. A woman with a short blond haircut and an earpiece in her ear popped her head out, smiled, and waved us forward.

Carina took my arm. "Just stay close."

"Okay, who *are* you?" I demanded as she pulled me across the sidewalk and past the eager fans. Some of them yelled at us and cursed as we slipped past them into the store. Others actually used their phones to take our picture.

"Carina! I'm so glad you're here. He'll be so excited you decided to come," the blond woman said to Carina as she led us through the shop.

"I'm really here more for Tess," Carina said. "Tess, this is Faith. She's Adam Michel's personal publicist. Faith, meet my friend Tess."

"It's nice to meet you, Tess," Faith said. "And thank you for getting Carina down here."

I stared at Carina's profile, but she refused to look at me. Suspicions were starting to eat away at the back of my skull, but none seemed able to form themselves into a coherent thought.

The line went right down the center aisle of the small store, ending at a table in the back where Adam Michel himself sat, smiling up at a fan as he signed her book. I almost tripped at the sight of him, my breath catching in my throat, and forgot all about the Carina weirdness. It was really him. Adam Michel. Sitting not five feet away from where I was standing. His dark hair was spiked up in front, and he wore a black leather jacket and his dozens of signature necklaces. His black eyeliner was perfectly applied, and his fingernails were painted a deep purple. I'd had this man's poster on my wall since I was in third grade and had seen him perform on a zillion different awards shows on TV. I couldn't believe I was now breathing the same air as him.

Faith left us near the corner of the table and slid behind it, leaning down toward Adam's ear from behind his shoulder.

"Adam!" she said quietly as he handed over the book. "Look who's here."

He looked up, and his whole face lit up. "Carina! Sweetheart!"

Carina smiled. "Hi, Daddy."

• • •

So. I got Adam Michel's autograph. And a half dozen pictures with him. And then we all had lunch together in the back room of the bookstore after he was done signing about three hundred books. I found out he doesn't drink soda, because he thinks it's poison. That all the rumors about him having a foul mouth were untrue. And that he had a daughter my age whose last name was Granger (Michel was a stage name), who he'd mostly kept secret, until it had leaked a few weeks ago on some gossip site along with a picture of the two of them swimming in St. Bart's. I had somehow missed this, but it was the reason Carina hadn't wanted to come to the bookstore. She'd always tried to stay out of the spotlight, and didn't want to lose her right to privacy now.

But she'd made this one appearance. For me.

"Thank you," I told her as Phil drove us back to the Lodge. "I really can't thank you enough."

"It was my pleasure, honestly. Also, it made him happy, so it's a win-win."

I couldn't believe I'd met Adam Michel. I couldn't believe I was now friends with Adam Michel's daughter. Lauren was going to lose her mind over missing this, and Christopher was going to freak out when I showed him the list.

My heart thunked. Christopher.

I took out my phone. Maybe this was the way to get through to him. To show him I was still working on the list. Would it hurt his feelings, though, to know I was doing it without him?

I thought of my mom and remembered. This wasn't about him. But I still missed him. I didn't want him to think back on this whole thing and hate me, either. I texted him.

Missed you today. Hope you're having fun at your cousins'.

I put the phone facedown in my lap and counted to one hundred. When I looked at it again, my face flushed. No response.

Normally, this wouldn't upset me much, because I don't necessarily expect everyone in the world to be looking at their phone twenty-four seven. But I *knew* Christopher was. He had almost nothing else to do with his time.

And suddenly, I wanted him to know that I was still on my mission, with or without his help. I wanted to show him that he *hadn't* derailed me.

I scrolled through my photos and found a shot of me and Adam holding up his book and sent it to Christopher.

#7 Complete! Wish you were here!

I didn't care whether or not he'd think that last comment was sarcastic. Really I didn't. This time I put my phone away, refusing to watch for a response. One more item down, only four more to go.

TESS'S NEW YEAR'S BUCKET LIST

1. Make a paper airplane that actually flies (20 seconds at least) ✔
2. Sing in public ✔
3. Strike up a conversation with a stranger ✔
4. Wear high heels outside the house ✔
5. Make out with a guy whose last name I don't know (???)
6. TP someone's house
7. Get Adam Michel's autograph ✔
8. Get a short, stylish haircut
9. Ski a black diamond slope ✔
10. Eat sushi

CHAPTER FIFTEEN

I went to the gingerbread house–building contest, hoping to see Loretta. I just wanted to make sure she was okay. And that she didn't entirely hate me. It wasn't like her not to get in touch for the whole morning, and I was starting to worry. Maybe this lawsuit thing was eating away at her. Maybe it was even more serious than I feared. Besides, after meeting my idol and getting more than halfway done with my list, I was feeling magnanimous. I could do this for Loretta. Maybe it would even cheer her up. Maybe it would even help the two of us *make* up.

The competition started at three o'clock, and we were home from the bookstore in plenty of time. I texted Lauren first in an attempt to guilt her into meeting me there, but she did not respond. Carina, however, was surprisingly excited about the prospect.

"I've never done anything like this before," she said, clapping her hands giddily as we walked into the spice-scented meeting room. "Being a rock star's daughter doesn't leave a lot of time for traditional projects like this. Most Christmases we didn't even have a tree."

"That's so not cool. Not even on the tour bus? A little fake one?"

She shook her head. "My dad did have one tattooed onto his leg one year when I complained, though. Said we'd never be without one again. Does that count?" She raised an eyebrow at me, and I laughed. "Anyway, thanks for bringing me here. It's so cool!"

I had to agree. Little stations had been set up around a half dozen tables, each with the pieces for constructing a modest-sized house, along with bowls and bowls of colorful candies to use in decorating. I saw bags of multicolored frosting at each chair as well, and remembered how my dad used to like to squirt it directly into his mouth, making it difficult to get any sort of cohesive design scheme going. It was a fun memory, but it also might be nice to build a gingerbread house without having someone there to eat the possibilities.

"I don't see Loretta, though," Carina added, rising up on her toes to search the room.

She was right. My grandmother was nowhere to be found. A few aproned lodge workers were corralling the guests, showing them to their stations and helping them get started, but Loretta was not among them.

"Maybe she's running late," I said, glancing at my phone. Still nothing from Lauren. Or Christopher for that matter. "Come on. Let's grab seats."

We took two chairs next to each other at a relatively empty table, and I showed Carina how to use the white royal icing to cement the walls of her gingerbread house together. While we were working, I noticed that Damon was one of the worker bees roaming the room, stopping to help whenever someone flagged him down. He caught my eye and smiled, and I smiled tentatively back. I wasn't entirely sure how I felt about Damon at this point. I wondered what he would say if I asked him point-blank what had happened with Christopher. Was it odd that he hadn't brought it up, considering he knew that Christopher and I were friends? Did he even know about the lawsuit?

"Hey! How're my two favorite ski bunnies?" Damon asked, stepping up behind our chairs.

Carina and I exchanged a look. "What is this, the nineteen seventies?" Carina said. "You can't call girls that."

"Sorry." He raised his hands. "How are my two favorite people? With whom I have gone skiing?"

"Better," I replied with a nod. "We're fine. We're going to build the coolest gingerbread houses here."

"I don't know." He shook his head. "Felicia over there has mad skills."

He nodded across the room toward an old lady with purple hair who was already putting a second story on her house. It looked like it was going to be a high rise.

"Wow. I cannot compete with that," Carina said.

"You don't have to. You're a rookie," I told her, and squirted some icing down the side seam of a corner on my house.

"We missed you at the party last night," Damon said to me.

The party. Right. I had temporarily spaced on that. "Oh, sorry. Turned out I was pretty exhausted after the skiing and the almost-dying." I threw that last part in for good measure, hoping it would make him back off.

"Got it," he said. "Well, we have a second chance, anyway. One of my friends from school is having a party at his house tonight on the other side of town." Damon leaned his hands on the backs of our chairs and hovered his face between ours. "His parents are away, so it should be pretty epic. Are you two ladies in?"

"Do you guys have a party every night around here?" I asked, incredulous.

"It's holiday break." He shrugged and smiled. "Besides, what else is the point of working at a ski lodge?"

I didn't exactly follow his logic there, but I let it slide.

"What about when you're in school?" I asked.

"What's school?" he and Carina both said at the same time, perfectly straight-faced.

"Oooookay," I said with a laugh, and attached another wall to my house. It was kind of amazing that my type A self had found the two most not-type-A people in the world to hang around with. I looked around for Loretta again, half wishing she were here to rescue me from having to say yes or no to this party. She must have had something planned for me and Lauren tonight, not that I could remember what it was. But there was still no sign of her. The clock over the door read 3:30. I had just over thirty-two hours to complete the last four things on my list. Maybe there would be sushi at this party? There would certainly be guys whose names I didn't know that I could potentially smooch with, though the very idea gave me the sweats. I considered Damon. We'd already kissed once. Maybe I could just get it over with, with him.

How very romantic.

Although, there was one other thing.

"How close are you with this guy throwing the party?" I asked.

He stood up straight and crossed his arms over his chest, making his biceps flex attractively, I couldn't help noticing.

"Pretty close," he said. "I've known him since kindergarten. He once helped me get a marble out of my nostril. After he'd shoved it up there, naturally."

Carina and I locked eyes again and laughed. "Charming," Carina said.

"Random question: Is he the type of person who would mind if we TP'ed his house?"

Damon laughed. "Mind? He'd probably love it. Dude, he'd probably help."

Carina eyed me curiously. "TP his—"

I gave her a pointed look, and her eyes lit up. "Oh . . . right! Brilliant!"

"Why do I have a feeling you two are leaving me out of something here?" Damon said.

"Because we are," Carina told him.

"Text me the address and time," I said. "And I'll be there."

"Me too," Carina said. "Sounds like fun."

"Perfection!" Damon said with a grin. He took out his phone and texted the details right then and there. "See you tonight."

He moseyed away, still tapping on his phone.

"I kind of love that he didn't even ask me why I wanted to TP his friend's house."

"Hey, I have a question. Why *do* you want to TP his friend's house?" Carina asked flatly. She had taken a handful of M&Ms and was popping them into her mouth one by one. She and my dad would have definitely hit it off. "Why is that an item on this all-important list? No, actually, I don't want to know. What I *do* want to know is why you started this list in the first place. Why call it a bucket list?"

I took a breath and put down the piping bag. Carina had already helped me cross off two of the biggest items on my list, so really, she was already a part of this. Plus, if I wanted to finish

it off before tomorrow night, I could use her help. If she was up for it.

"You know how some people make new year's resolutions?" I began.

"Ugh, I hate that tradition. If you want to change something about your life, just change it. Why do you have to wait for an arbitrary holiday to do it?"

I smiled. "Exactly."

And then I told her the whole story.

• • •

Damon's buddy, Chase, lived on a quiet street on a hill, a small house on a large piece of property with trees dotting the front yard. Mature trees, my mother would have called them. Which made the place perfect for toilet paper. Lauren, Carina, and I had bought a few packages on our way over, making our Uber driver stop at the little drugstore in town. But Damon had gone all out. He'd shown up with a trunk full of discount toilet paper and a half dozen friends who were super excited for the task. So while some people were inside doing the normal party stuff, and others were hanging out on the front porch watching, Carina, Damon, and I, along with his rando friends, were going to town with the TP.

"This is completely ridiculous," Carina said, pulling her arm back with a full roll of toilet paper in her hand. "And I *love* it!"

"I don't know why I haven't been doing this my *entire life*!" I shouted, tossing streamers over low-hanging branches all around me. I held a long string of paper above my head, executed a very ungraceful spin move, and flung it. It fluttered and floated and

landed on top of the mailbox. Inside the house, music pumped and somebody screeched, then laughed. Clearly the party was as fun on the inside as it was on the outside.

"Probably because you'd get arrested." Lauren, who was sitting on the front porch under several blankets and sipping from a red Solo cup, kept offering sarcastic commentary. She had chosen not to participate, and instead to film the entire thing on her phone. Tarek had to work tonight, so she was flying solo, which had made her a bit more subdued. She leaned over toward the girl sitting next to her and explained, "We live in a very lame suburban town."

"Well, they'd arrest you here, too," Damon offered from above, "if we didn't have the homeowner's permission."

I looked up into the high branches of the biggest oak tree on the lawn. Damon had strapped an entire twenty-four-pack of two-ply onto his back and was now sitting up there, looking quite comfortable, TP-ing the tree from the inside out.

"I like your technique," I told him.

"Thank you. I thought it was rather genius myself." He smiled and tossed another roll toward the ground. "Plus I like the view from up here. I can see all the stars."

I tipped my head back even farther. It was a gorgeous, clear night and the deep purple of the night sky was completely blanketed in pinpricks of light. You could never see stars like this where I was from. Chalk up a point in the "pro" column for Vermont.

"Do we *have* the homeowner's permission?" Carina asked, stepping out from behind the tree's trunk. "Because if I get arrested, my father will murder me. Or maybe buy me a puppy." She looked me in the eye. "He has a rather unpredictable parenting style."

I laughed, making a huge cloud of steam with my breath, and flung more toilet paper.

Damon lifted his shoulders. "Well, technically the home-owners are away, but we have their son's permission."

Carina and I exchanged a look. "Good enough for me," I said, and she giggled.

"Let's go deal with that little shrub over there," she suggested, pointing. "It looks lonely and bare."

"I'm in."

We tromped across the front lawn, the frost-covered grass crunching under our boots. There had been no natural snow in these parts for days—all the snow on the ski trails was manmade—but it was plenty cold. I had my hat pulled down all the way over my ears and forehead, and my fingers were frigid even inside my gloves. I wasn't going to last out here much longer.

"You take that side and I'll take this side," Carina suggested.

I complied, and then we launched our toilet paper, but the shrub was so small, Carina's roll hit me dead in the face.

"Oops! Sorry!" she said, cracking up.

I picked up the roll. "No problem!" I said, and launched it right back at her. It pinged off her shoulder and went flying, and then I was suddenly embroiled in an epic toilet paper fight. I ran to gather more rolls, Carina enlisted backup, and before long a couple of guys had joined her team and I found myself wrapped up like a toilet paper mummy and begging for a truce.

"Okay, okay. Let her go, men," Carina said, waving off the pair of Damon's friends who had joined her team. I busted out of the toilet paper wrap rather easily, and we stood back toward the street to check out our handiwork.

"Not bad," I said, taking off the gloves so I could blow warm air into my hands.

"This is basically the most normal thing I've ever done for fun," Carina told me. "Well, this and the gingerbread house making."

"Wait, seriously?" I said. "Why? What do you normally do for fun?"

"I don't know . . . I travel a lot, so whatever's going on where I am. I played roller hockey basketball a couple of weeks ago, if you can imagine that. And I had a hot pepper–eating contest with a WWE wrestler. Oh, and for my birthday we went to Bali, and my best friend and I got matching butt tattoos."

Okay. I was basically the lamest person ever. Here I was, trying to get outside my comfort zone and do something crazy, and my crazy thing was the tamest thing Carina had ever done. I mean, butt tattoos? Seriously?

"I know what you're thinking, and yes, I totally regret the tattoo."

"Not at all what I was thinking," I said, my insides burning with thinly veiled humiliation. God, she must have thought I was such a loser. I looked around at the entirely toilet-papered front yard, of which I'd been so proud just moments ago, and kind of wanted to set fire to the whole thing.

Then, Carina put her arm around me and squeezed. "Thank you, Tess."

"For what?" I asked, baffled.

"I've always wanted a normal-kid existence." She smiled at me wistfully. "This has honestly been more fun than any of that other stuff. And I wouldn't have done any of it without you."

My heart flipped and I smiled, mood changed on a dime.

"You're welcome," I said. And my chest swelled a bit. My list had gone beyond me to make Carina's life a little better, too. Just like, for a hot minute, it had made Christopher's life a little better.

I tugged out my phone to check for messages. I hadn't even thought about Christopher since we'd been here, but he would have really loved this one. Still nothing from him, though, and my spirits sunk.

But I wouldn't let them sink entirely.

"Come on. Let's take a picture of this."

"Abso-freaking-lutely!" Carina said.

She leaned in as I angled a selfie so that we could get the big tree in the background, and I captured the shot. Just like earlier, I fired it off to Christopher with a text:

#6 Complete! Still wish you were here!

• • •

TESS'S NEW YEAR'S BUCKET LIST

1. Make a paper airplane that actually flies (20 seconds at least) ✔
2. Sing in public ✔
3. Strike up a conversation with a stranger ✔
4. Wear high heels outside the house ✔
5. Make out with a guy whose last name I don't know (???)
6. TP someone's house ✔
7. Get Adam Michel's autograph ✔
8. Get a short, stylish haircut
9. Ski a black diamond slope ✔
10. Eat sushi

...

An hour later I was dancing. With Damon and Chase and two of their other friends whose names I couldn't remember. Lauren was schooling some guy in a basketball game on the Xbox, and Carina was nowhere to be seen, but I was pretty sure she was in the kitchen showing people how to make her famous microwave tacos.

Damon slipped his arms around my waist and pulled me in close so that our bodies felt like one connected thing. I blushed and tried to pull away, but he held me tighter, and I felt the need to look up. To see if I could figure out exactly what he was thinking. But when I looked up, his eyes were closed, his head tipped back as he danced.

Miraculously, I still didn't know his last name. I could just kiss him. Right here, right now. I could kiss him and cross #5 off my list. It was looming closer and closer to midnight with every passing second. Soon I'd have only twenty-four hours to finish my list. This might be my last chance.

I was just about to grab his neck and pull him toward me when a bright white light hit me dead in the eyes, blinding me to everything. A scream pealed out from very nearby, and then someone pounded on the door. Three hard, serious knocks.

"This is the police! We're shutting this party down!"

And then, all hell broke loose.

Suddenly I was on the floor. And it wasn't until I looked up and saw Damon running for the back door that I realized he'd shoved me. On my shoulders I could feel where his hands had pushed me away from him. Then, someone stepped on my fingers, and I shouted. People were careening everywhere. My sister threw the Xbox controller onto the hardwood floor, where it shattered in ten pieces.

"Tess!? Where are you?"

"Down here!" I shouted, waving my injured hand.

She lunged for me as everyone else scattered.

"Are you okay?" Lauren asked, dragging me up.

"Yes. No. I don't—Damon threw me on the freaking floor!"

"I know! I saw him. Jackass. I hope you didn't hook up with him," Lauren said, pulling me toward the back door.

Really? That's what she was thinking about right now?

"Open the door or we're busting it down!" someone yelled.

But then, impossibly, they were inside. Two cops streamed in from the back entry, shining their flashlights in everyone's faces. Lauren took a quick turn and dragged me toward the staircase, where I saw Carina standing, frozen like one of the ice sculptures back at the lodge.

"Come on!" Lauren cried, trying to pull me upstairs.

"What? Why? What good is that gonna do?" I demanded. "Are we going to jump out a second-story window?"

And then a hand came down on my shoulder. I was turned roughly around, and a cop with a skinny moustache held his phone up next to my face. "Yep. This is her."

What? What were they talking about? Her *who*?

"I've got one of the other ones," another guy said, hand clasped around Carina's arm.

"I'd let go if I were you," she said. "I have a very famous father, and he has two dozen lawyers on emergency retainer."

"Yeah. Right, kid," the cop said with a smirk. "Let's go. Outside."

They half shoved, half dragged us out the front door. Lauren made a desperate sound, and I knew she was trying to decide between running with the rest of the party and following us to make sure I was okay. As much as I wanted her by my side, I kind of wanted her to run. She didn't need to get in trouble, and if she left, she could get Loretta.

God, Loretta. The last time I'd seen her, she'd called me a child to my face, and now I'd gone and proven her right. She was going to lose her mind when she found out about this. But what even *was* this? There were dozens of kids at the party, and I hadn't even drunk anything. Why were they zeroing in on me and Carina?

Then, we made it to the porch, and I knew. The other cops

had corralled Damon and two of the friends who had helped us in our toilet paper mission. Even now, the front yard looked sort of beautiful, all that white paper fluttering gracefully in the breeze under a blanket of twinkling stars. Though the flashing red and blue lights of the three police cars did muck it up a bit. The cops forced us down onto the porch steps next to the other perpetrators. I couldn't even look at Damon. My ribs still hurt from where I'd hit the floor when he'd pushed me.

"Are these the kids who toilet-papered this property and yours?" one of the cops asked.

My brow scrunched, confused. Then a wizened old man stepped out from behind the line of blue-clad officers. He looked us over one by one and then nodded. "Yep. I caught it all on video, as you've seen."

"Wait, we didn't do anything to *his* property," Damon said, earning a *shhhhh* and a kick from the friend on his other side. "What? We didn't! We only TP'ed Chase's house, and he said it was okay."

"Well, young man, I happen to know that the Hansens are in Florida right now, so I don't see how you could have gotten their permission to do this to their property," the old man said, hitching up his pants with both hands.

"Oh, I don't know, cell phone? Text? Email?" Damon said. "What year are you living in?"

"Would you shut up?" Lauren spat from behind us.

"You should probably listen to your friends, there, kid," Skinny Moustache said.

Damon hung his head, muttering something unintelligible under his breath. Though I swear I heard my name in there, and I was sure I heard the words "stupid idea."

"What part of your property was compromised?" the officer asked the old man.

"That tree over there," the old man said, gesturing at the small shrub Carina and I had attacked last. "That little tree is on my side of the property line."

Carina and I exchanged a rueful look. If only we hadn't decided to decorate that last little shrub. But how were we supposed to know it wasn't on Chase's property?

"What if they offer to fix your tree?" Lauren suggested.

"No way! We didn't touch that tree! That was the girls!" one of the other kids cried.

Oh my God, I hated these people.

"Well you're the ones who supplied the toilet paper!" Carina countered.

"But it was *her* idea," Damon said, nudging me with his knee.

"You said it was okay! That Chase said it was fine and that was enough!" I cried.

Suddenly we were all yelling at once. I couldn't believe this was happening. I'd just wanted to have a teeny bit of fun. Kids my age did stupid, dangerous, even life-threatening stuff every damn day and never got caught, but the one time I stepped my pinky toe out of line I had cops manhandling me and yelling at my friends.

It was too bad I didn't put *Get arrested for doing something dumb* on my bucket list.

Suddenly, a whistle pealed. I winced, and everyone fell silent. "All right. All of you. Up! Let's get you down to the station. We'll sort it out there."

The boys began to protest, but Carina, who was clearly so over this, just got up, lifted her chin, and walked directly toward the line of police cars parked on the street. I looked back at Lauren, giving her my most pleading eyes.

"Don't worry. I'm on it," she said. "I'll be right behind you."

Feeling a heavy dread unlike anything I'd ever felt before, I joined Carina at the police car at the front of the line. "I'm *so* sorry about this," I said. "Do you really think your dad is going to be that mad?"

"Please. Do you know how many times me and his manager have had to bail *him* out of jail?" She scoffed. "It's about time it was the other way around."

And I never would have thought I could have smiled right then, but I did.

· · ·

It took a ridiculously long time for the police to get our forms filled out with our names, ages, and addresses, and to take our statements. Throughout the whole thing, I alternated between being so nervous I could barf, and feeling straight up angry. This was all so unfair. There had been so many underage kids there who were drinking—actually breaking the law—and here we were getting booked for misuse of toilet paper. What a world.

Parents began to trickle in, and everyone got a stern talking-to before being let off with a warning. When Adam Michel arrived, the clerk at the front desk asked for a selfie, and Adam immediately obliged, telling his assistant to post it and hashtag it #babysfirstarrest.

"Dad!" Carina protested. "I wasn't arrested!"

"It'll get *so* many likes, though," her father replied, giving her a noogie.

Carina lifted a hand in my direction as she ducked her head and was escorted by her dad's security detail out the back door.

"See you soon, Tess!" Adam called back to me.

And I swear the looks on everyone else's faces *almost* made this whole debacle worth it. Adam Michel knew my name. Ten-year-old me was doing cartwheels.

Tarek showed up to pick up Damon. Which was weird, since everyone else had parents to pick them up. But maybe Damon's parents were currently away. He looked *so* angry when he signed his cousin out, his jaw set and his eyes sharp.

"Lauren told me what you did to Tess. Are you freaking kidding me?" he snapped.

"What do you mean? I didn't do anything to her! It's her fault we all got dragged down here!" Damon replied.

"This is the last straw, Damon. I swear," Tarek said. "Let's go. Mom and Dad are waiting."

Damon looked like he was about to argue, but Tarek stared him down until he walked out the door. I felt a lot more relaxed with Damon gone from the little holding cell they were keeping us all in. Having to sit next to him all that time until Tarek showed up had made me itch all over. I was so glad I hadn't had the chance to kiss him. Who cared about the damn list? I didn't want a guy like that anywhere near me. And now I didn't even have to count our small kiss on the slopes, because I knew his last name. He'd given it to the cops when they were filling out the forms. Dumas. Pronounced *Doo*-mas, but easily revised into Dumb Ass, if you asked me.

Loretta was the last to arrive. Which was fine, because I needed a little time to myself to chill.

I stood up from the uncomfortable metal bench the second Loretta strode through the door. It was after midnight, and she wore actual jeans under her wool coat. That was a shock. I couldn't believe the woman even *owned* jeans. But more surprising was the sight of her face without any makeup. It was like looking at a ghost version of my powerful grandmother. Her skin was pale and wrinkled, her eyes seemed to retreat into her head without her usual eye makeup, and her lips were very thin. I almost wouldn't have known it was her, except she took the same businesslike, nononsense tone with the officer who greeted her, as she did with everyone who worked for her.

"I don't see why all this drama of coming down to the station was necessary, Officer Peele," she said as she signed the paperwork to release me. "If you were going to let them off with a warning, you could have simply done so at the house."

"Well, ma'am, we wanted to make sure this was an experience they wouldn't soon forget," Officer Peele said, hooking his thumbs into his utility belt.

"I think that the educating of children falls to the parents, Officer Peele, don't you?" she said. "Please tell Chief Harrison to call me. I'd like to have a few words with her. And you'd better hope I'm in a better mood then, or I'll be filing a formal complaint." Officer Peele turned purple and nodded mutely. Then Loretta snapped her fingers at me and waved at the door. I scurried out ahead of her, joining Lauren, who was waiting in the small square lobby area.

Loretta stepped up behind us, tugging on a pair of leather gloves and pulling her keys from her wrist bag. Her hands were shaking, and she dropped the keys on the floor with a clatter. I bent to retrieve them and held them out to her. My heart felt like lead.

"I'm really sorry, Loretta," I said sheepishly. My voice was like a squeak.

"I don't want to talk about this now." She looked at the keys for a moment, then turned to my sister. "Lauren, you'll drive home. I have a sudden splitting headache."

"Yes, Loretta," Lauren said.

Then Loretta slid between us and out the door into the frigid night air.

"I think I broke our grandmother," I said.

Lauren took the keys and put her arm around me, giving me a quick squeeze. "Let's just get her home."

• • •

The ride back to Evergreen Lodge felt miles longer than the Uber trip we had taken to get out to Chase's house just a few short hours earlier. Loretta spent the entire drive with her eyes closed and the bridge of her nose pinched between her thumb and pointer finger. When Lauren attempted to turn on the radio, Loretta simply tsked, and Lauren turned it right off again.

I sat in the back of the car, feeling like the worst piece of sludge ever to grace the planet. Not only had I not so much as seen Loretta all day long, but then we'd dragged her out of bed with a call from the police station. What must she have thought when she'd picked up the phone to hear it was the Evergreen PD calling? What must have gone through her head? It was no wonder she had a splitting headache.

Lauren kept glancing at me in the rearview mirror, and I was sure my expression mirrored her own. We were both worried. Not just about what Loretta might do to us tomorrow, but about Loretta. She'd never been silent for this long. At least not that I had seen.

My phone pinged and I flinched. Who the hell would be texting me now? Maybe Carina, letting me know whether or not she was going to be grounded?

"Will you kindly turn that off?" Loretta bit out, eyes still closed from what I could see in the side mirror of the car.

"Sorry, Loretta."

I fumbled with my phone, turning it over to hit the power button, and saw that the text wasn't from Carina. It was from Christopher.

My heart began to pound. Finally. He was finally responding! I opened the text, not daring to imagine what it might say.

> Wow! I can't believe you met Adam Michel. That's so cool Tess!

Tears pricked at my eyes. It had been a long day. And I had been so worried I'd never hear from him again. After everything that had happened, this olive branch felt like exactly what I needed. Then, the three dots began to scroll again, and I quickly turned off the sound on my phone so Loretta wouldn't hear when the next text came in. I watched and waited for what felt like hours. Finally, his next text appeared.

> Listen, I can't do this anymore. I shouldn't be talking to you. Good luck with the list

Wait. What? He wasn't serious. I started to text him back, but then the three dots popped up again.

> Sorry. Hope you have a good new year

Wow. And I'd thought this night couldn't get any worse.

CHAPTER SIXTEEN

DECEMBER 31

An insistent knocking at our hotel room door woke us up the next morning. I cracked one eye open and glanced at the digital clock on the table between our beds. It was 7:45 a.m. I couldn't even believe I'd fallen asleep. For most of the night, I'd stared at the ceiling, going over and over the night and trying to figure out what I could have done differently. Not said yes to the party, for one thing. Not trusted Damon when he'd said TP'ing Chase's house would be fine. Not putting the toilet paper prank on my list to begin with. If only I could go back in time.

But no such luck.

I put my pillow over my head and groaned, hoping the person at the door would just go away, but they kept knocking, and Lauren finally threw a pillow at me.

"You're closer to the door!" I griped.

"You're the reason we didn't get to bed until three a.m.!" she replied.

She had a point. I threw my covers off and stomped over to the door, checking through the peep hole. When I saw who was on the other side, I stood up straight, my heart skipping a terri-fied beat.

"It's Loretta," I whispered urgently.

Lauren sat up, her hair covering half her face. "What?"

"And she looks like herself again!"

"Girls!" Loretta barked, but still in a low enough voice that she wouldn't disturb the other guests. "I can hear that you're whisper-ing in there. Open the door."

Lauren shrugged at me like, *What else can you do?* So I took a deep breath and opened the door. Loretta's eyes flicked over my pajamas before she stepped into the room, flipping on the light and nearly blinding the both of us. Lauren threw a hand up and squeezed her eyes closed for a second before blinking them against the onslaught.

"We are going to have breakfast in the Overlook. Just the three of us. I want the two of you to meet me there at eight-thirty sharp." She glanced around the room where both of us had shucked off our clothes into piles before climbing into bed last night. No one had brushed their teeth, washed their face, or thought about being tidy. Didn't Loretta realize we'd only gotten to bed less than five hours ago? Hadn't *she* gone to bed less than five hours ago? "We are going to be spending the day together, so I suggest each of you showers quickly and makes yourself presentable. I will see you in forty-five minutes."

She strode out the door, closing it quietly behind her, and Lau-ren flopped back onto her bed with a sigh.

"I guess I didn't break her after all," I said.

• • •

The Overlook was a small, very expensive restaurant on the top floor of the lodge, with a wall of floor-to-ceiling windows looking out over the mountains. The view was absolutely breathtaking, and with the windows facing east, we were able to watch the sky change colors as the sun rose higher behind the hills. Of course, it was nearly impossible to enjoy nature's light show, because I was so dang nervous that Loretta was going to tear me a new one right there in front of all her wealthiest guests.

I shouldn't have been worried about that, though, because Loretta's main goal in life was to make sure her guests had a perfect vacation. They weren't to experience a moment of unpleasantness while staying at Evergreen Lodge.

The waiter placed our breakfasts in front of us. My silver dollar pancakes were presented in a perfect stack with a toothpick down the center that was topped by a Christmas tree. The tower was surrounded by strawberries cut to look like little Santa hats, with a dot of whipped cream at the tip of each to represent the white fluffy ball on top. Lauren's scrambled eggs were more elegant, since I guess her meal was considered something adults would eat. Loretta had a yogurt parfait and coffee.

"This is way different from the buffet," Lauren said, placing her napkin in her lap.

I did the same and removed the toothpick from the pancakes, causing them to topple over. Half fell on the plate, while the other half hit the white tablecloth. Loretta's eyes narrowed. Hands shaking, I quickly tossed the pancakes back onto my plate.

"Sorry, Loretta. Sorry."

I folded my hands in my lap, afraid of what I might do if I touched the ceramic pitcher of syrup.

"Girls, there's no reason to be nervous," Loretta said. "I invited you here to apologize."

Lauren's gaze darted to mine. "You . . . apologize to us?" she said. "What for?"

Loretta rested her wrists against the edge of the table and looked down at her food for a moment, as if gathering her courage. My stomach clenched. For a second I thought she was going to apologize to me for dismissing my concerns about the lawsuit, but no. This felt bigger than that. It felt like some life-altering revelation was coming all of a sudden. What was she going to tell us?

Then she lifted her eyes and looked at each of us in turn.

"I'm sorry I wasn't there for you more as you were growing up," she said. "I wasn't there much for your father, either, when he was young. If I had been . . . if I had done some things better, maybe everything would be different right now. For you. For your mother. I'm afraid I was selfish when your dad was young and he . . . he's possibly living up to my example."

Her eyes filled with tears, which was even more disturbing than seeing her tired and makeup-free last night.

"What?" I said. "Loretta, no."

"You can't blame yourself for Mom and Dad getting divorced," Lauren put in. "That's on them."

"Seriously," I added. "This stuff happens. I think Mom and Dad . . . I think they just sort of . . . grew apart."

Lauren looked at me, her expression sympathetic. I don't think I realized I understood what had happened until I said it, but it was true.

"They want different things now," Lauren put in. "There's no way your having a career when Dad was a kid made *that* happen."

Loretta reached for Lauren's hand, which was in her lap, and squeezed it. Then she reached for mine across the table, and I gave it to her. Her fingers were bony and cool, but somehow comforting when they took mine.

"You girls are very kind," she said. "And I'm sorry that you have to go through all this." She released our hands and folded hers in her lap again. "But whatever has happened in the past, there's no reason we can't get to know each other now," she continued. "For example, I would very much like to know what possessed you to sneak out to a party and throw toilet paper all over some stranger's front yard."

My heart thunked. But Loretta picked up her spoon and dug into her breakfast as if this was nothing more than a casual conversation. I looked at Lauren, who raised her eyebrows at me.

"That's all you," she said, and cut into her eggs.

"I . . . just . . ." I reached for the syrup pitcher and fiddled with it. "It was just something I always wanted to do. I mean, when you see people do it on TV shows or whatever, it looks like so much fun."

"And was it? Fun?" Loretta asked.

"It actually was," I said with a wan smile. "Until the police came."

"Oh, come on, Tess," Lauren said. "If Loretta wants to get to know us, don't you think you should tell her why you're really doing all this stuff?"

I shot her a death glare, but Loretta sat up a bit straighter, intrigued. "What stuff are we talking about?"

"Singing karaoke, making paper airplanes, going off to meet Adam Michel—"

"Well I could have introduced you to Adam Michel," Loretta said. "He's one of our VIPs this week."

"She has this list," Lauren said, leaning in. I kicked her under the table, but she didn't even flinch. All those years of playing soccer, I guess. "It's a list of things she wants to accomplish before the new year."

One of Loretta's perfectly plucked eyebrows arced, and she looked at me. "Really? How interesting."

I felt hot all over, suddenly. "It's not. It's stupid, really." I picked up the syrup and poured it all over my pancakes. I didn't want to talk about the list. Especially since it was now officially impossible for me to complete it. What random guy was I going to find to make out with before the end of the day?

"It's not stupid," Lauren said. "I think it's the coolest thing you've ever done."

"Really?" I said, and couldn't help smiling.

"Well, today's the last day of the year," my grandmother informed me, as if I wasn't already very well aware. "Have you completed it yet?"

I shook my head and speared the tiniest pancake. "There are still three things left on there."

Loretta put her spoon down and leaned in, giving me a conspiratorial grin. "Then we'd better get to it. Where do we start?"

I was about to pull the list out of my bag when a shadow fell over the table. We all looked up, and my jaw dropped. It was Tarek and Damon. Tarek looked determined, and Damon was staring at his feet.

"Tarek?" Loretta said. "Is everything all right?"

"No, it's not, Mrs. Sachs," Tarek said. "And I'm sorry to interrupt your family meal. But there's something Damon wants to show you."

It was a video. That much Lauren and I got before Loretta shut the office door in our faces and we were forced to sit outside with Frank while she met with Tarek, Damon, and her lawyer.

"What is going on?" Lauren asked. "Why is the lawyer in there?"

"Um . . . yeah. There's something I should probably tell you," I said, and sat down on the small couch.

By the time I was done with the story of Christopher's accident and his accusations against Damon and the lawsuit and the fact that Christopher had bailed and wasn't speaking to me, Lauren's jaw was on the floor.

"I knew it. I knew there was something about that kid that I didn't like," Lauren fumed.

"Yeah, I know," I said, then blinked. "Wait. Which kid?"

"Damon!" she said, throwing a hand toward the closed office door.

"You thought he was cute! You thought I should make out with him!"

"Yeah, but I also thought he was shifty." She narrowed her eyes.

"Okay, remind me never to trust your taste in guys," I said.

Then the office door flew open, and the lawyer came striding out, cell phone to his ear. "Yes, I'd like to speak to Phillip Mosure, please. It's about the Evergreen Lodge case."

We were still smelling his aftershave when Damon shouted, "You're *firing* me?" from inside the office.

"Yes, I'm firing you," Loretta said. "We'll mail you your last paycheck in the new year."

Damon muttered something else, then stormed out, walking right past me and Lauren without so much as a glance. A couple of seconds later, Tarek came out, looking sheepish, and stepped over to Lauren.

"Sorry about all this."

"Are you okay?" she asked. "You're not fired, too, are you?"

"No. At least, not at the moment." He looked chagrined. "I gotta take Damon home. Call you later?"

She nodded, and he gave her a quick kiss, then left.

"Girls! Come in here, please!" Loretta called out.

We exchanged a wary look, then went inside.

Loretta was behind her desk, looking shell-shocked.

"Ummm . . . what just happened?" I asked.

"What just happened was Tarek and Damon showed me video of Damon shoving your friend Christopher clear off one of our trails and laughing when Christopher slammed into a tree," Loretta said, somehow keeping her voice completely even. "He has been fired, and the lawyers will hopefully come to a settlement. One that, if there's anything they can do about it, won't bankrupt this place."

"Oh my God, Loretta. Is that even possible?" Lauren asked, bringing her hands up to cover her mouth.

"It's possible. But I'm hoping cooler heads will prevail. This is unbelievable. Truly." She turned her back to us for a moment and her shoulders shook. Was she crying? My chest felt so tight I could burst.

"You know this isn't your fault, right, Loretta?" Lauren said.

When Loretta turned around again, her eyes were wet, but her makeup was intact. "It *is* my fault, Lauren. The people who work for me . . . I'm responsible for them. I stood up for Damon. Innocent until proven guilty and all that. But now, well, he's been proven guilty."

"What made him show you that video?" I asked.

"He's had some issues, it seems, with acting out. Tarek said something about his parents being away all the time." Loretta shook her head. "Maybe this is his way of trying to get their attention. It's a shame. I feel sorry for the boy."

"For Damon?" I blurted out.

Loretta looked me in the eye. "Nothing is black and white, Tess. And appearances can be deceiving. You never know what's going on in a person's life unless they tell you themselves. Remember that." She gathered her purse and took a deep breath. "Well. Shall we?"

"Shall we what?" I asked, confused.

"We still have your list to complete, Tess," she said. "And I believe I just made a promise to you girls to spend more time with you, did I not?"

Okay, was she out of her mind? She just had a huge bomb dropped in her lap and she wanted to go get my hair cut?

"Loretta, no. You're going to have so much to deal with. We don't have to—"

"Nonsense. There's nothing I can do at the moment but wait for the lawyers to call me. In the meantime, I will need a distraction."

"Seriously?" Lauren and I said at the same time.

"Seriously," Loretta replied, giving a nod toward the door. "Now let's do this thing."

. . .

Chunks of hair fell on my shoulders and back, then slid off the slippery black cape I was wearing and tumbled to the floor. The stylist had turned my chair away from the mirror when I'd gasped at the first snip, and hadn't turned me back since, but I could still *feel* it happening. And, though I was mostly keeping my eyes squeezed shut, every now and then I'd sneak a peek at the floor. There were mountains of hair all around the chair. Mountains. How could all of that possibly have come from one person's head? From *my* head?

"This is amazing," Lauren said, forcing me to open my eyes and look at her. I immediately wished I hadn't. She had my phone, and was training it on me, walking from one side of my face to the other.

"Are you *filming* this?" I demanded, distraught.

"Trust me. You're going to be *so* glad I did," she said with a laugh.

My cheeks burned. Was that a mocking laugh? Or a delighted laugh? Which was worse? I mean, mocking would be bad, but maybe she was delighting in the fact that I was going to look like a freak when all of this was over.

"Would you please stop?" I asked.

She must have heard the desperation in my voice, because she did. She sat down in the chair next to Loretta's a few feet away and started scrolling through the pictures on my phone. Loretta wasn't currently in her chair, though, because she was busy in the next room, alternating between socializing with Marika—the older and very retro-looking woman who owned this chic salon—and speaking urgently into her phone. I could only imagine she was consulting with her lawyers.

"Excuse me, but that's *my* phone," I said to Lauren.

"Yeah, and you've taken more pictures in the last week than you have in the last month," she said, not even looking up. Her finger kept flicking away. "Guess that's what happens when you get a life. Aw! Look at this one!"

She turned the screen toward me, displaying the selfie Christopher and I had taken after our successful paper airplane experiment. There was an acidic feeling in my stomach.

"Oh, he's cute," said Glen, my stylist, pausing momentarily in his work. "Boyfriend?"

"Um, no," I said.

"Christopher should be here for this," Lauren said. "And I'm sure he'd want to hear about the whole Damon-being-fired thing. I still can't believe that jackass."

"Have you heard from Tarek?" I asked, half wanting to know and half wanting to simply change the subject. "Do you have any idea why he showed Loretta that video?"

"He didn't tell me. But he seemed pretty pissed off at Damon after the whole toilet paper incident." Lauren shifted in her seat. "And I may have told him how Damon shoved you to the floor."

"You did?"

"Uh, yeah I did. You're my sister and he should know his cousin's a jerk." She stopped scrolling on my phone momentarily. "But you know what? He didn't seem all that surprised. Just mad. My guess is he forced Damon to come clean somehow."

"Wow. Kinda harsh, making your own flesh and blood turn themselves in," I said.

Lauren grinned. "Tarek has a good moral compass. It's one of the reasons I like him." She blushed, and it was almost too sickening to witness. It hit me that I was jealous. She had an actual relationship happening, and I had zip.

"So . . . what exactly happened with Christopher?" she asked. So much for changing the subject.

"I told you this morning," I said. "He left. He went to visit his cousins yesterday and he's not coming back."

"Are you sure he's not coming?" Lauren asked.

"That's what his parents told me." I was going to lift my shoulders, but worried that would result in my ear getting clipped by the shears. "I think he's mad at me—for going skiing with Damon. And I got the feeling he wasn't exactly comfortable hanging around the lodge while his parents were suing the place. I guess he didn't like me enough to stick around."

Lauren gave me a *You know better than that* look.

"What?" I said.

"Um, please. That boy is *totally* smitten with you, Tess. It was written all over his face every time he looked at you."

"That sounds promising," said Glen, resting a hand on my shoulder.

"Well, even if he did like me, I'm never going to see him again."

"That's a shame, because with this haircut, you're going to look like a supermodel," Glen told me. Then he put down his shears and picked up a blow dryer, effectively cutting off any further conversation.

And my sister started to scroll on my phone again. I decided to close my eyes and pretend that none of this was happening.

After a few minutes of blowing and using some sort of weird gel stuff to muss my hair, Glen stepped back to look at his handiwork.

"Amazing," he said. "A complete transformation."

Lauren looked up, and her jaw dropped. She stood up, lifted my phone, and snapped a picture, then did the same with her phone.

"Loretta! You have to see this!" she called.

My grandmother appeared at the doorway, her phone against her ear, and her free hand went up to cover her heart. "I have to call you back," she said into the phone, and ended the call.

"Is it that bad?" I asked.

Glen tsked.

"You look gorgeous!" Loretta said. "Glen, turn her around so she can see herself!"

Glen spun my chair, and there I was. Except it wasn't me. It was an older me. A more sophisticated me. A me with cheekbones and incredibly stunning blue eyes. Where had *those* come from?

"He's right, Tess. You look like you could be in the pages of *Vogue.*"

Then Lauren started to tap away at my phone.

"What're you doing?" I asked, panicking.

"I'm sending the picture to Christopher," she said. "He should know what he's missing out on."

• • •

"Where shall we go for lunch?" Loretta asked once we stepped out onto the sidewalk. My whole neck felt cold and tingly, and I turned up the collar on my coat. I was going to have to become a scarf person with this haircut.

"Is there a Japanese place nearby?" I asked.

"Yes! We can go to Yuki. And it's so close we can even walk there." Loretta turned and started to walk down the hill. Lauren and I fell into step behind her, Lauren basically gaping at me the entire time.

"Will you stop?" I asked, trying not to smile.

"I'm sorry. It's just . . . it's amazing. You look like an entirely new person."

I took out my phone—noticing that there were no messages from Christopher—and turned the camera so I could see myself. My reflection was really going to take some getting used to. It was unbelievable how much the shape of my hair had changed the shape of my face.

"You should FaceTime Mom. She won't even know who you are."

"Oh my God, you're right. Let's do it!"

Loretta paused at a street corner, waiting for a light to change, and I quickly called my mother, holding up the phone so she could get the best view of the new me.

"Hi, Tess. What a lovely sur—"

She stopped and her face froze. For half a second I thought the call had dropped. But then she screamed.

"Oh, my goodness! You cut your hair!"

"I did! What do you think?"

"Sweetie, you look beautiful!" my mother cried, tears in her eyes. "Oh, honey, you look so much *older*." She covered her mouth with her free hand. "Oh, I wish I'd been there."

I felt a pang, but tried to shove it aside. "I know. I'm sorry. I just felt like if I didn't do it today, I was never going to do it."

"You don't need to apologize. Was this on your list?"

"Yep!"

My mom waved a hand in front of her face, trying to fan the tears away. "I just love it so much. I can't wait to see it in person."

"Well, you will in a couple of days," I reminded her. "Thanks for giving me the confidence to go through with it," I added, my heart full.

"Anytime, kiddo. Boys are going to fall all over themselves for you with that haircut."

"Whatever, Mom," I said, and rolled my eyes with a laugh. Loretta had already crossed the street and was waving us over, standing in front of the Yuki sign. It was the corner restaurant on the opposite side, and I could see the long counter where people lined up to select their sushi rolls, just like in a movie. "I have to go. We're going to try sushi!"

"What!? No, you are *not*."

I was crossing the street as my mother said this, and Lauren shot me a confused look at my mom's alarmed tone.

"Don't even joke about that," Mom said.

"Wait . . . what do you mean?" I asked. "Joke about what?"

"Tess Sachs, you cannot have sushi." My mother's face was pale and stern. "You're allergic to shellfish!"

"I'm *what*?"

I looked at my grandmother. "Well . . . of course you are, dear," Loretta said, stricken. "I assumed you wanted to come for some chicken teriyaki or something like that. You can't have fish. Or, at least, any fish that might have come into contact with shellfish."

"Wait, wait, wait." Lauren grabbed the phone from me and looked at my mother. "Are you seriously telling me that Tess is allergic to shellfish? How do I not know this?"

"Forget you! Why do *I* not know this?" This was insane. My mother wasn't with me twenty-four hours a day. What if I had tried lobster at a friend's house? Or eaten the gross crab cakes at school?

"Why do you think we never, ever eat fish? Never go to seafood restaurants?" my mother said. "You girls *know* this."

"But we've had fish sticks . . . right?" Lauren asked, looking completely confused.

"Yes, but only ones that are safe for shellfish allergies," Mom said, clearly exasperated.

Lauren and I locked eyes over the phone. I threw up my hands and she shook her head.

"Mom, neither of us knew this," Lauren said.

I grabbed the phone back again.

"Okay, will you girls stop doing that?" my mother said, hand to her forehead. "You're making me dizzy."

"Mom, I am sixteen years old. How have I gotten through my entire life not knowing I'm allergic to shellfish?"

"I honestly have no idea. You really don't remember that time you ate a lobster roll on vacation and your whole face swelled up and you could barely breathe? We had to give you, like, a bottle of Benadryl before you even started to go back to normal."

"That was because of the lobster?" I asked.

"What did you *think* caused it?"

"I don't know, Mom! I was six!"

She took a deep breath and let it out. "Well, I'm sorry if the message didn't get through to you, sweetie, but you absolutely cannot have sushi. There's no way to guarantee there's no cross-contamination. I'm so glad you called me."

"I wouldn't have let her eat it, Abigail!" my grandmother called out.

"Thank you, Loretta!" my mother replied, but raised her eyes to the heavens on the screen. "Tess. Go get a burger for lunch," she told me. "And call me later so we can say Happy New Year."

I swallowed hard against a suddenly dry throat. "Okay, Mom. Love you."

"Love you, too, kid. And you really do look beautiful."

"Thanks."

I hung up the phone and shoved it away. Every muscle in my body sagged. I trudged to the nearest bench and sat down heavily. Both Lauren and Loretta walked over to stand in front of me.

"Well, that's it, then," I said. "Even if I gave myself a pass on number five, I can't finish the list. I can't try sushi."

"Can't you simply revise the list?" Loretta asked.

I unzipped my backpack, slipped the list out, and handed it to her. "It's laminated."

"But the list really only exists in your mind, doesn't it?" Loretta asked. "Why not just come up with something to replace numbers ten and five? Which, by the way, I disapprove of mightily, I might add. Whyever would you want to make out with some boy you barely know?"

Lauren snorted a laugh. "That was supposed to be Damon, before he turned out to be the biggest jerk ever."

"Well. I'm glad you didn't go there," Loretta commented.

"Me too," I replied.

I bent forward at the waist then, realizing anew that my whole list project was down the tubes. Loretta was right, in theory. The list really only existed in my mind. There were probably two other things I'd never done in my life that I could complete before tonight. But that just felt wrong. And it partially felt wrong because Christopher wasn't here. He'd inspired me to make the list. He'd helped me write it in the first place. He'd been there when I'd laminated it and when I'd crossed off the first item. I wondered if he knew, yet, that Damon had confessed. Suddenly, I really just wanted to talk to him. He would help me figure out what to do. But it was pretty clear from his texts last night that he was done talking to me.

I lifted my head and looked at my family.

"Come on," I said morosely. "Let's just go get a burger."

TESS'S NEW YEAR'S BUCKET LIST

1. Make a paper airplane that actually flies (20 seconds at least) ✓
2. Sing in public ✓
3. Strike up a conversation with a stranger ✓
4. Wear high heels outside the house ✓
5. Make out with a guy whose last name I don't know (???)
6. TP someone's house ✓
7. Get Adam Michel's autograph ✓
8. Get a short, stylish haircut ✓
9. Ski a black diamond slope ✓
10. Eat sushi

CHAPTER SEVENTEEN

Sitting in the back seat of Loretta's car, I wished I could just go back home right then. I needed this trip to be over. But all that was waiting for me back home was a house without Dad. I wondered how much would look and feel different without him there. Had he taken all his old movie posters out of the basement? Would we still have the pasta bowls he always bragged he'd bought on sale when he was a bachelor? I was certain he'd taken his favorite backyard BBQ apron. The one that read "Sauce Me" on the front. I never really knew why that was funny, but he always loved it.

Loretta and Lauren were chatting about Lauren's travel plans for next year—Loretta listening for once instead of constantly shooting down all of Lauren's ideas. I took out my phone and put it faceup in my lap. Part of me felt like a loser for continuing to try. Especially after last night's message from Christopher and the fact that he hadn't replied to the picture of me Lauren had sent him. But I had to let him know that the whole list experiment had crashed and burned. It was over. I felt like he somehow deserved to know.

I snapped a pic of the unfinished list and sent it to him, followed by a message.

Epic fail. Couldn't get #5 and #10 done. Had a good run, though. Turns out I'm allergic to sushi. Who knew? And #5, well . . . I think that one is just not my style.

I stopped typing and blinked back tears, holding my breath. Should I tell him? It might break my heart if I told him and he didn't reply. Again. But if I didn't tell him, I was pretty sure I'd always regret it. I let the breath go, and just went for it.

I like you Christopher. And I'm sorry if I did anything to hurt you. I just thought you should know that before New Year's. Thanks for inspiring me. I may not have finished the list, but I wouldn't have done any of it without you.

I hit *Send*, then turned my phone off and leaned back in the seat, closing my eyes until we got back to Evergreen Lodge.

• • •

That night, I lay on my bed and stared at the ceiling while Lauren got ready for the New Year's Eve party. I felt like such a failure. Maybe it had been too much to take on—ten things I'd never done before in five days. Maybe I should have come up with five. But come on, it wasn't like I'd added "travel around the world" to the list, or put "have a baby" on there, or even "skydiving."

Skydiving. My heart gave a pang. I looked at my phone, which I'd tossed on the desk when I'd come in earlier. But I refused to turn it on. I didn't want to know for sure that he hadn't texted me back. I wasn't sure I could take that kind of disappointment right now.

The bathroom door opened, startling me, and steam poured out. Lauren, wrapped in a towel, stared at me.

"You're not getting dressed?"

"I'm not going," I told her, flopping down flat again.

"You can't not go," she told me. "It's New Year's Eve!"

"It's just another night," I told her, which made her groan. "Besides, I don't have anything to wear. The nicest thing I brought with me are my black jeans."

"Wear something of mine!" she said. She strode across the room, flung open the closet, pulled out three dresses—she'd hung something up?—and laid them across her unmade bed. There was one purple halter dress, one red dress with a plunging back, and a black strapless thing I could never even imagine wearing.

"You would look *amazing* in this," she said, holding up the black dress. "With your new haircut?" Her eyes shone as she walked over to my side of the room. "Stand up."

"Lauren," I whined.

"Stand. Up."

I knew that when she got in this mood there was no denying her, and I had no energy to argue. I pushed myself up and let her hold the dress up in front of me. Her smile widened.

"You don't even need heels! You can wear your black ballet flats and you'll look gorgeous."

She shoved the dress at me so that I had to take it. I wrapped one arm around it and let it fold over, the hanger dangling toward the floor.

"I don't do strapless," I told my sister in a flat voice.

"Great! It'll be one more thing you've never done before that you can get in before the new year!"

Lauren brushed past me, pulled my list out of my bag, grabbed my Sharpie, and crossed out *"Eat Sushi"* before I could stop her. I gasped as she wrote next to it, *"Wear a strapless dress to a party."*

"Lauren! You can't just edit the list!"

"Huh. That's funny. Cuz I just did." She popped the cap back on the pen like a punctuation mark, then tossed it on the desk and walked back into the bathroom. "Put that on and then I'll do your makeup."

She slammed the bathroom door.

I stared down at the list. All that laminated perfection. All my perfect little check marks in a row. And now she'd gone and scribbled all over it. But then again, it was never going to be actually perfect. It was never going to have ten check marks. My genetics had made sure of that. Maybe this should be one more bucket list item—stop obsessing about perfect to-do lists. Start being a little more flexible.

I walked over to the full-length mirror on the back of the hotel room door and held the dress up against my body. The flouncy skirt would hit just above my knee. I was sure the bodice wouldn't fit—my sister was much curvier than I was—but if we could figure out a way to pin it . . .

"Fine," I grumbled to myself.

Nine items down. One to go. And even in my grumpy mood, and even though it wasn't perfect, the thought made me smile.

• • •

"This isn't half bad for a, quote, *teen party*!" Carina shouted in my ear as we danced in the middle of a crowd of sweaty people.

"I know, right?" I replied, executing a twirl so the skirt on my borrowed dress flared out. I couldn't believe how crowded it was. I hadn't seen this many kids my age around the lodge all week. Where had they come from? Whoever they were, I'd caught a few of them glancing at my hair or doing double-takes as I walked by, which meant I'd been blushing half the night. I felt pretty. I felt like I was being seen for the first time.

"Are you having fun?" Lauren asked, joining us.

"I guess," I said, glancing at the door.

"You have to stop doing that!" she shouted at me.

"Doing what?"

"Watching the door," Carina put in. "If he shows, he shows. But you'll look *much* cooler if you're not staring at the door when he does."

Lauren lifted her hand and Carina high-fived her. I rolled my eyes. "Whatever. I'm not waiting for him. He's not coming back. And even if he did, why would he come here? He can't dance. If he even tried to step on the dance floor, he'd basically get killed."

"Woo-hoo! It's the hottest girls in the room!"

Lauren stopped dancing and shot a look over my shoulder, just as Damon wrapped his arms around me from behind. Just the scent of him—coffee and gum—made my stomach turn. I whirled around and shoved him away from me with both hands. He stumbled backward into a group of kids dancing behind him, and one girl squealed as she spilled her soda.

"Sorry!" I shouted to her, though I wasn't sure if she heard me.

"What's your problem, Tess?" Damon said. He was wearing an

open-collared button-down shirt and pants that were too tight. His hair, normally back in a ponytail, hung long over his shoulders. It was longer than mine now. I didn't like it down. It made him look much older and, weirdly, skeevier.

"My problem? What are you even doing here? My grandmother fired your ass!"

"So, I snuck in. So what?" he shot back, like he could not understand what the problem was. "Why are you freaking shoving me into people?"

"Are you seriously asking me that right now?" I turned my palms out. "Do you not even remember what happened last night?"

"Last night?" he said. "You mean when you and your stupid prank got me and all my friends dragged down to the police station? And then I got in trouble with my aunt and uncle, and Tarek told on me to Loretta as punishment. Yeah, I remember that. That was *awesome*. But I forgive you."

My jaw hung open, my face heating up as I realized we were starting to draw attention. The people dancing closest to us had stopped and turned around to stare. A couple of them were even filming on their phones. Carina took a few steps back, and I knew it was because she didn't want to get caught on social media in the middle of a melee. My sister, though, stepped up right behind me.

"You shoved me to the floor the second the cops showed up and basically let me get trampled," I said. Okay, I was exaggerating, but just a little. That was how it had felt at the time. "And then you blamed the whole thing on me."

"It was your idea!" he blurted out.

"Yes, it was my idea. But you said it was fine! You got Chase's okay, you bought the toilet paper, you helped us do it." I shook my head. "But you know what, forget all of that. You also *purposely* knocked my friend off the slopes and broke his leg. Do you think I'd really want to talk to you after that?"

"Not likely!" Lauren chimed in.

"I don't like you, Damon," I added, crossing my arms over my chest. "And I'd appreciate it if you would go away."

Damon took a breath. He looked like he was about to say something else, but then he glanced around at our audience, at their phones, and something shifted on his face.

"Whatever. You're not worth it, anyway," he said to a chorus of "Oooooh" and "Burn!" Then he turned and walked away.

"All right, everyone. Show's over. Go back to what you were doing," Lauren said to the crowd, adding a shooing motion with both hands. Carina rejoined us as everyone went back to dancing, and I felt my shoulders relax.

"That was awesome," Carina said.

I glanced at the door again. Couldn't help it. But there was no Christopher. Is it wrong that a little part of me was hoping he had seen that? That he'd arrived at the exact right moment to witness me telling off Damon?

My sister reached out and squeezed my hand. "Maybe it's for the better that he's not here," she told me. "You don't want to kick off the year with someone who's not for real."

I couldn't argue with her logic. I had really liked Christopher for those first few days. But this whole ghosting thing he was doing now? It wasn't right. I didn't deserve to be treated this way. I deserved to surround myself with people who cared about me.

"I'm glad you guys are here," I told Lauren and Carina.

They both hugged me, one from each side, mushing me between them.

"We are, too," Lauren said, releasing me.

Carina threw her arms in the air. "Now let's dance!"

• • •

And we danced. But then we got tired. Or at least I did. It had been a long few days, not to mention an exhausting twenty-four hours. At this time last night I was being hauled off in a police car for the very first time. I guess the stress of that and then sitting in the police station for hours and then getting into a fight with my grandmother, getting up early for breakfast, and having my hair lopped off had taken a lot out of me. With a few minutes left until midnight, I was sitting at a table, slumped so low in the chair my butt was hanging of the edge, and I really didn't feel like celebrating. Lauren and Carina were still on the dance floor, taking selfies with props they'd stolen from the photo booth—huge sunglasses, paper crowns, fake moustaches—and I saw the opportunity to make my escape.

With their backs to me, I got up and slipped toward the perimeter of the room, sliding past raucous dancers and edging my way by the dessert table.

"Only eight minutes left until the new year!" the DJ announced, and everyone cheered. He'd been doing that every sixty seconds for the past half hour, and it was making me tense. I got to the door and could taste my freedom, feel my pajamas on my skin, when a hand wrapped around my wrist and stopped me short.

"Carina!" I cried.

"You are *not* leaving this party before midnight," she admonished me.

I glanced past her for Lauren, but she was still on the dance floor, wearing her crown, dancing with Tarek. At least they weren't teaming up on me. Carina, I could handle.

"Come on! Is this all because of that list!? So, figure out something else to do!"

"Like what?" I asked.

Her eyes went wide, incredulous.

"There must be loads of things you've never done before." She looked around the room as if the answer was going to pop up in front of her. "I don't know . . . moon a party? Do ten cartwheels in a row? Go streaking?"

"Okay, (A) I'm not doing any of those things, and (B) Do we need to talk about the fact that two of your three suggestions involve partial to full nudity?"

She laughed. "Come *on,* Tess. You can't go back to your room alone to ring in the new year. The very thought of it makes me depressed."

"The thing is, Carina, I like being alone." I pulled her in for a hug. "I'm fine. I swear," I said, though I could feel my voice wanting to crack. "I really do just want to go to bed. I appreciate it, though. I really do."

I kissed her cheek and pulled away, looking into her eyes. "Happy New Year!"

"Happy New Year," she said grudgingly.

And she let me go.

I tucked my chin and walked down the carpeted hallway, marveling at how the ridiculously loud music quickly became nothing more than a thumping beat. My ears rang from all the noise, and my heart felt full. Inexplicably, my eyes welled with tears. Maybe I should go back. Maybe Carina was right and I shouldn't ring in the new year alone.

But it felt too late to turn back now. I'd be okay. As soon as I got to my room, I'd feel better.

I just wished . . . I don't know what I wished. That I'd finished the list? That Christopher had texted back? That any of this had turned out the way I'd imagined it would?

One tear slipped out as I reached the lobby. And then, I heard my name.

"Tess?"

I looked up, and there was Christopher.

TESS'S NEW YEAR'S BUCKET LIST

1. Make a paper airplane that actually flies (20 seconds at least) ✓
2. Sing in public ✓
3. Strike up a conversation with a stranger ✓
4. Wear high heels outside the house ✓
5. Make out with a guy whose last name I don't know (???)
6. TP someone's house ✓
7. Get Adam Michel's autograph ✓
8. Get a short, stylish haircut ✓
9. Ski a black diamond slope ✓
10. ~~Eat sushi~~ Wear a strapless dress to a party ✓

CHAPTER EIGHTEEN

He was standing right next to his couch, the fire roaring in the fireplace behind him. On the coffee table where we'd rested our hot chocolates while we pored over the list, there was a bottle of champagne and at least a dozen glasses. In fact, there were champagne bottles and glasses all over the room, the staff having prepared for every guest at the lodge to have a chance at a New Year's Eve toast.

"Hey," Christopher said, his eyes taking all of me in. "You look . . . amazing."

I blushed. "So do you," I said. Christopher was wearing a suit. An actual suit with a light blue shirt under it and a dark blue tie. Plus he was standing—no crutches—balanced on one foot. Standing up straight for the first time since I'd known him. And from what I could tell, we were exactly the same height.

"What're you doing here?" I asked.

At the same time he said, "I'm so sorry, Tess."

I took a few steps toward him, my heart pounding like mad in my chest. "Sorry for what?"

"For everything," he said. "I only left because my parents didn't want me talking to you anymore. They said since you were a member of the family that owned the lodge, it wasn't . . . *prudent* was the word they used, I think. They were worried I'd say something that would mess up the lawsuit or whatever. And they didn't want me texting you, either."

"Oh. I guess that makes sense," I said, both stung and at the same time relieved. He hadn't been avoiding me because he wanted to. He'd been avoiding me because he was ordered to.

"And I was a little mad, too, if I'm being honest," he said. "It was awful seeing you with that guy. I don't even know how to describe it."

"I understand," I said. "Especially now that I know what he did. But I never liked him, Christopher. You have to know that. I never even remotely thought about him that way. It was always—"

I stopped, realizing what I was about to say. The word *you* was on the tip of my tongue.

"Always?" He grinned, and reached for my hand.

"Yeah," I said. "Always."

He ran his thumb across the top of my knuckles, and I felt that touch in every last inch of my body. I couldn't believe this was happening. I couldn't believe he was here.

"Wait," I said. "Why are you here?"

"I got my parents to drop the lawsuit," he said.

"You did?"

He tilted his head. "Well, settle the lawsuit. All they really wanted was for Damon to be fired and my medical bills to be paid. So once Loretta let him go, I talked them into dropping the ridiculous number they'd come up with for 'psychological trauma' and asking only for the money to cover the hospital and stuff. Which I think is fair."

"Totally fair. Oh my God, Christopher. Thank you!" I let go of his hand and threw my arms around him, but the force of my hug sent him off-kilter, and we both went tumbling backward over the arm of the couch.

"Ow! Oof!" Christopher said.

"Oh God!" I crawled away from him and jumped up, careful not to touch his cast. He was sprawled awkwardly on the cushions, his good leg still hooked over the arm. "Are you okay?"

"I'm fine, I'm fine." He straightened himself out until he was sitting on the couch and I was standing in front of him. He looked up at me, pushing his now mussed bangs away from his eyes. "Hey . . . whatever happened with the list?"

"Oh, I'm not going to finish it," I said, waving a hand, the humiliation hitting me in a fresh, new wave.

"Why not?" he asked. "I mean, I got your texts, and texted you back, like, a hundred suggestions of things to replace five and ten."

"You did?" I asked, gleeful.

"You didn't get them?"

"I turned off my phone."

He covered his face with his hands. "Oh, come on, Tess. You have to finish!"

I glanced at the clock. "There's literally two minutes left. I mean, I already wore a strapless dress to a party to replace the sushi thing, but what can I do in two minutes that's epic enough to be worthy of the list."

"I don't know . . . dance on a table?" he said, gesturing at the coffee table, which was still full of glassware.

"Yeah, that's not happening." I looked at him and an idea occurred to me. "Wait, what's something *you've* never done?"

His eyes widened. "Me?"

"Yeah. I only did this whole thing because of you. You've been a part of it from the beginning. Give me something good," I challenged. "Something I can do on your behalf."

"Are you kidding? This is too much pressure. I can't—"

"Let's start the countdown!" the DJ at the teen party shouted, his voice reverberating down the hall and into the lobby. All the well-dressed adults milling around us began to murmur and pick up glasses, pouring out champagne and toasting.

"Twenty! Nineteen! Eighteen!"

"Give me something! Anything!" I said to Christopher, waving my hands.

"Uh . . . I don't know, I don't know!" he said.

"Seventeen, sixteen, fifteen!"

"Christopher!" I prodded.

"Fourteen! Thirteen! Twelve!"

His eyes lit up. "I've got it!"

"Ten! Nine! Eight!"

He reached up his hands to me and I pulled him to standing— pulled him up hard enough that we bumped chests.

"Seven! Six! Five!"

Christopher looked into my eyes. We were so close our noses were practically touching. We really were the exact same height.

"Four! Three! Two!"

His breath was warm against my mouth as he said, "Ever kiss a guy wearing a cast before?"

My heart skipped as I realized what he was saying. I smiled, my skin tingling from the tips of my ears to the tips of my toes.

I closed my eyes, and I kissed him.

"One!"

Fireworks exploded outside the windows. Literal fireworks to mark our first kiss. But they may well have been inside my chest.

"Happy New Year, Tess," Christopher said, his lips against mine.

"Happy New Year, Christopher."

TESS'S NEW YEAR'S BUCKET LIST

1. Make a paper airplane that actually flies (20 seconds at least) ✓
2. Sing in public ✓
3. Strike up a conversation with a stranger ✓
4. Wear high heels outside the house ✓
5. ~~Make out with a guy whose last name I don't know~~ ~~(???)~~ Kiss a guy in a cast ✓
6. TP someone's house ✓
7. Get Adam Michel's autograph ✓
8. Get a short, stylish haircut ✓
9. Ski a black diamond slope ✓
10. ~~Eat sushi~~ Wear a strapless dress to a party ✓

EPILOGUE

—

SIX WEEKS LATER

"It's really happening?" I asked Christopher, holding my phone up so he could see my face as I shoved my feet into my newish Vans. He was sitting on an exam table at the doctor's office, the paper sheet crinkling beneath him every time he moved.

"It's happening!" he said gleefully. And maybe a little fretfully. Not that I could blame him. Some person was about to come at him with a circular saw. "Distract me while they get this thing ready," he said, clearly trying not to glance at the doctor, who was off-screen. "What are you doing today, Type A?"

"I'm going to meet Jenna and Liam at the skate park," I told him. "I told them I'd get them ollying before spring."

Jenna and Liam were the ten-year-olds I was teaching how to skateboard. After returning home from our winter break trip, I'd gone straight to the indoor skate park downtown and signed up to give beginner lessons. It had both forced me back onto my board and introduced me to a lot of new people. Plus, I was making bank. Parents, it turned out, paid a good chunk of change for their kids to be entertained for an hour—and to learn a new skill.

"That's awesome. Tell them I said, 'hey.'" Christopher had met Jenna and Liam briefly during our second class, when I'd FaceTimed him to prove I was skating again. Not that he didn't believe me. I just liked to keep him informed. I'd also called him after my first French club meeting, and when I'd gone with Lauren to volunteer at the animal shelter. I was trying new things all the time now. Some had worked out better than others (don't get me started on the glass-blowing class), but I was really enjoying putting myself out there. Although I was kind of shocked at how long it was taking for my right eyebrow to grow back. Fire was not my friend.

"What's your latest new thing?" I asked. "Aside from getting your cast off?"

I heard the saw fire up in the background, and Christopher gulped.

"Well, I bought my first train ticket to Philly," he said.

I almost dropped the phone. "You did?"

Christopher's parents hadn't let him come visit me yet, because they were worried about him navigating mass transit with his cast and crutches. But we'd been hoping they'd let him come visit once he got the cast off.

"I did!"

"Okay, time to hand the phone off," said a voice off-screen.

Christopher handed the phone to someone else, and for a second I just saw the ceiling lights and something blue, but then I was focused on Christopher again.

"You there?" he said, squeezing his eyes shut.

"I'm here!" I shouted, hoping to be heard over the buzz of the saw.

He opened his eyes after the blade first hit the plaster and watched until the cast was completely free, a big grin on his face. As soon as it came away, I cheered, and Christopher sat up to better see his pale and shriveled skin.

"It's still there!" he joked, looking at me.

"Well, that's a relief," I joked back. "Think you'll be ready to try skateboarding when you come out here?"

He gave me a wry look. "Sure," he said. "Add it to the list."

"You know I will!" I said, shooting him an air kiss.

And you know I did.

CHRISTOPHER'S POST-CAST BUCKET LIST

1. Buy a ticket to Philadelphia ✓
2. Learn to ice-skate
3. Ride a unicycle
4. Kick a real field goal
5. Go to a 76ers game
6. Dance with Tess
7. Go on a bike ride with Tess
8. Go swimming with Tess
9. Go hiking with Tess
10. Go skateboarding with Tess

ACKNOWLEDGMENTS

Thank you so much to my amazing editor, Wendy Loggia, for bringing me back into the Penguin Random House fold. I had so much fun working on this book, and I couldn't be happier to reunite with one of my earliest working partners. Special thanks go out, as well, to my fellow author and loyal cheerleader, Jen Calonita, as well as to my family, who were kind enough to give me alone time here and there so I could bring Tess and Christopher to life. Finally, thank you to everyone at Underlined for all the hard work you've done on this novel. I can't tell you how much I appreciate all that you do!

DON'T MISS ANOTHER GREAT ROMANCE FROM UNDERLINED!

1

Christmas Wrapping

I should realize it's a bad sign when I trip hard over the entry to Winslow's Bookshop.

"Whaaaaa!" I yelp as I give the typically sticky front door my customary push . . . and unexpectedly go flying into the store, the shop's brass bell announcing my unceremonious entrance.

"Carl finally put a little oil on that door so we don't have to work so hard to get in here," Victoria, the owner of Winslow's, says, looking up at me with a bemused smile. Nothing ruffles her. She's on her knees, putting a stack of books on a wooden shelf. "Hope you didn't hurt yourself."

My eyes dart around. Luckily the only people to witness my epic fall are Victoria, who has the decency not to laugh in my face; a mom preoccupied on her phone while pushing a baby stroller; and Victoria's basset hound, Fred. He gazes balefully at me, a pair of reindeer antlers perched on his large head.

"Nope, I'm fine." I take in a deep breath. "Ahhh, my favorite smell: peppermint, pine cones, and new books." I'd started working at Winslow's last summer, and despite what my friends who lifeguarded, camp-counseled, and taught dance thought, bookselling was the best summer job ever. I've actually been lucky enough to stay on part-time during the school year. Victoria and her husband, Carl, own the bookshop and they are supercool. Everyone who works here loves to read and talk about books. Winslow's is a popular place in our town for people to come and spend time. It is, as Victoria likes to say, a community.

Victoria is always encouraging us to take books home to read. "Read more, sell more," she'll say, handing me copies of the latest romances (my favorite). The store also runs a mystery book club and an award-winner book club, and it has tons of events for kids. There are strands of twinkly lights, comfy chairs filled with pillows, old wooden bookshelves worn smooth from years of use, and a café in the back that sells the most delicious panini and acai bowls and gives us a 20 percent employee discount.

If I could live here, I would.

Victoria stands up, a pair of pink tassel earrings swinging from her ears. "You're not scheduled to work tonight, are you?" she asks, her brow puckering.

I shake my head. "Wrapping." I've been averaging around ten hours a week at the store this fall, but tonight I am here strictly in a volunteer capacity. Each holiday season, Victoria and Carl invite students from my school, Bedford High, to staff the wrapping station and accept donations. All the money goes to support the arts at our school, and I'd signed up for a weekly shift.

"Ahhh, right." Victoria clasps her hands together. "Okay, off to special-order *The Atlas of Amazing Birds* for a young naturalist before I forget. Coffee's made in the back if you want a cup." She walks off. "French hazelnut," she calls over her shoulder before I can ask.

In the staff room in the back, I shrug out of my blue parka and pink scarf and pull out my light-up Christmas bulb necklace from my GOT BOOKS? tote bag.

"Ah, there she is, Miss Bailey Briggs, a cup of Christmas cheer." My coworker Bill bustles past me, a pencil behind his ear and a coffee mug in his hand, his standard white cotton shirt rumpled as usual. Originally from Ireland, and about the same age as my grandpa, Bill is as much a fixture in the store as the comfy sofas in the Fiction section and Fred at the cash register. And with his heavy Irish brogue, he is one of the most popular readers at Saturday Storytime.

"Hi, Bill," I greet him. "Did you finish that mystery you were reading last week? The one about a murder in Dublin?"

He chuckles. "I did, I did. Already on to the next in the series. I'm addicted, I am, Bailey. Tana French. You should give her a read."

I pull on my plush Santa hat and arrange my hair. "Not my thing, Bill. Sorry."

"I know, I know. You want what all the young girls want. A loooooove story." He gives me a dismissive wave.

Even though I find his attitude slightly patronizing, I have to admit he's right—at least when it comes to me. I *do* want a love story. Specifically, a Christmas one. A sweet one, filled with snuggles under blankets and hot chocolate and text messages filled with red and green hearts and Santa emojis. I've watched more than my fair share of Hallmark Christmas movies, and even though I'm not a big-city lawyer who has moved back to my hometown to save the family business or a world-weary writer who falls in love with a recently widowed baker, I still believe in the power of Christmas Magic.

A holiday romance is in my future.

At least a girl can dream.

And it isn't like I don't have something to back my dream up. I meet two of the main criteria for a cheesy Christmas romance:

1. I work in a bookshop.
2. I was dumped, although not that recently.

I dated Oliver Moreno for four months before I found out that he wanted to just "be friends" because he had kissed Kate Collins, a sophomore in the marching band. The kiss took place after the winter concert, and apparently it was life-changing.

Whatever. Oliver isn't that great a kisser, if I'm being honest. Kate can have him.

But see, that isn't the point. I don't just want someone

to kiss. I want someone to experience Christmas Magic with me. Christmas Magic begins the moment Santa appears at the end of the Macy's Thanksgiving Day Parade. That's when the holiday season always starts—the season of cookie baking and tree trimming, sledding and snowfalls, Secret Santas and eggnog and Christmas songs on every radio station. It really is the most wonderful time of the year.

And what I really want for Christmas is something I probably would never admit to anyone. Not to my friends, and definitely not to my sister. It's honestly hard to even swallow my pride and admit it to myself.

But here it is: I want to be kissed underneath the mistletoe by someone who really thinks I'm amazing.

That's it. That's my Christmas wish.

I don't think it's too much to ask for.

But will it ever come true?

• • •

"Snowmen or snowflakes?" I smile up at the college-aged guy standing in front of my gift-wrap station.

He doesn't answer me. Instead, he drops a heap of books on the table with a loud *thunk*. I pick up the top one. It's a cookie cookbook. "OMG, this looks delicious," I say, flipping to a recipe for salted chocolate chunk cookies. "Or should I say . . . *doughlicious?*"

My wrapping partner, Sam Gorley, laugh-snorts beside

me. "It must be time to go home, because I'm actually start-ing to find your jokes funny." She yawns. "Or maybe I'm just tired." Sam is in my grade at school. We aren't really in the same friend group—she hangs out mostly with the band kids—but since we started volunteering at the gift-wrap station, we've become kind of friendly. She spends a lot of time posting on social media and showing me pictures of her cat, Meow.

We've been wrapping for three hours now, and we're starting to get a little silly.

I turn back to the customer, who is staring at the giant rolls of wrapping paper. "So what'll it be?" I am very into themes, especially when they involve the holidays, and holi-day baking is one thing I'm always in favor of. So a guy buying a cookie cookbook as a gift makes me happy. Maybe he's going to surprise his girlfriend with homemade sugar cookies. Or maybe he has a little brother he wants to teach how to bake in time for Saint Nick. I smile, imagining the heartwarming kitchen scene.

He cuts me off mid-fantasy, frowning. "Uh . . . do you have something a little less . . . Christmas?"

I can't stop myself. I frown back. *Less* Christmas? Less Christmas is right up there with No-Egg Easter and Fire-crackerless Fourth, obviously a phrase that would never pass my lips, but I try to maintain my professional com-posure even though I'm wearing a plush red Santa hat and a strand of blinking lights from Five Below around my neck. "Oh, sure," I say smoothly, reaching under the table and hoisting up a roll of wrapping paper. The rolls are even heavier than they look. "We don't have room on the table for all our choices. Here's another Happy Hanukkah . . . and we also have Dogs in Stockings."

He shakes his head, his shaggy bangs covering his eyes. "Nah. How about something purple?"

I stare at him. "As in red meets blue?"

He nods. "Yeah. Purple."

I'm about to object when Sam awakes from her nap and whips into action. "Here you go, sir," she says, grabbing the books and wrapping them in a flurry of white tissue paper. She puts them in a fancy cream-colored WINSLOW's bag, slaps a gold foil sticker on it, and ties it up with a purple ribbon that she apparently pulled out of thin air. "Happy holidays!"

"Cool. Thanks." He pushes a couple bucks into the donation jar and heads out the door, the little bells dinging upon his exit.

Sam turns to me and holds up her hand in anticipation of what I'm about to say. "Don't even start."

My shoulders rise and fall. "I just don't understand people," I say sadly. "Purple? For Christmas?"

Sam's scrolling rapidly through her texts. "Not everyone's as into the holidays as you are, Bailey."

"So I've noticed," I tell her, dejectedly picking at the fuzz on my red wool sweater.

"Anyway, are you going to that party tomorrow night at Joe's house?" she asks, not looking up from her phone.

I shake my head. "I don't even know what you're talking about."

Sam sighs in the overly dramatic manner I've come to know well these past few weeks. "Joe Shiffley invited a bunch of people over to hang out. You should come."

I shrug. "Maybe." I don't even know Joe, so the idea of showing up at his house for a party feels very awkward.

No one is coming over to the gift-wrap table. Sam heads to the restroom, and while she's gone, I decide to rearrange everything. I line up the ribbon spools on the left—green, red, white, blue, silver—and put the tape dispenser next to them, along with a giant pair of scissors, a candle jar we now use to hold pens, and two gigantic rolls of paper. I pick up all the stray bits of cut ribbon from the floor and fluff the money in the donation jar.

When the bell at the shop's entrance rings, I glance over. And when I see who it is, my eyebrows shoot up. It's Jacob Marley, this guy from my grade at school. We were in biology together in ninth grade. The main reason I know him is because he had gone out with this girl, Jessica Dolecki, that I dislike. She has thick wavy blond hair, a pushed-up nose, and a high-pitched laugh, and she always wears a Canada Goose jacket. I think Jacob is on the track team—or maybe he's a wrestler?—but other than that, I don't really know him. He's wearing dark track pants, sneakers, a gray sweatshirt, and a Boston Red Sox cap.

He lifts his chin in my direction. "Hey, Bailey."

"Hey," I say back, giving him an awkward wave. I'm a little surprised that he knows who I am.

"Nice hat," he says, smirking. "Goes with the necklace."

"Why, thank you," I say, adjusting the white furry rim while ignoring the fact that what he said is most likely not a compliment.

"So, uh, you work here?"

I shrug. "I do, actually. But tonight I'm just here to wrap."

He laughs, and a dimple in his right cheek makes an appearance. "Never would have guessed you and Drake had something in common."

"I never would have guessed I'd see you in a bookstore on a Friday night," I retort before I can stop myself.

He shoves his hands into his pockets. "What's that supposed to mean?"

"Oh, um, I don't know," I say feebly, feeling my cheeks pinken. Why did I say that? He doesn't exactly seem like the reading type, but really, I don't even know Jacob. That sounded a lot meaner than I meant it to.

"So, yeah, I'm doing some shopping. For Christmas."

Something in my heart gives a little flip. Any boy who comes to a bookstore for Christmas shopping gets bonus points. Now I feel extra bad that I insulted him. Most boys I know give gift cards for presents—if they even give a gift. Oliver and I weren't together at Christmas, but something tells me he would definitely have been the gift-card type. Or, if I'm being honest, the no-gift type.

"And so you came in here," I say, stating the obvious.

He nods. "Would you want to help me?" He holds up his phone. "I've got a list."

"Oh," I say, surprised. "I mean, I'm not technically working now but . . ." Known fact about me here at Winslow's: giving people book advice is my thing. There's something about matching the right book with the right reader, putting the right book into a customer's hands: I love it. And helping a customer like Jacob is extra-satisfying, like watching my parents master a TikTok dance I've taught them.

I'm in.